CHAPTER ONE

I will always remember the first time I saw her. I knew instantly that I wanted her more than I ever wanted anything else in my life. What I failed to realize, then, was that she was going to change it irrevocably, and forever.

She was perfect, with the sleek lines of her body and posture, and with tail neatly placed on the ground, along the right side. I was certain that the small bronze statuette was representing the Egyptian goddess Bastet. Nurturing instincts were combined with boundless carnal lust in the "character" of the goddess. In ancient times, Egyptians worshiped and celebrated her dual nature, often represented in the shape of a cat. The statuette was at least 20 inches tall, the glazed material polishes to a shine, the eyes fashioned in yellow enamel. She had tiny gold hoops hanging from her pointed ears. I walked in, savoring the musky smell in the darkened shop. I blinked couple of times to allow my eyes to adjust to the dim lighting. Everything inside was covered in a thin layer of gray dust, creating giant heaps of items, whose outlines I could not really see. Coins, and several artifacts of a questionable authenticity, were scattered on the small counters. Half opened trunks were lined along the walls, colorful fabrics and rugs rolled or just thrown within. I moved in closer to the spotless side table the statuette was displayed on. She was absolutely flawless, even on closer inspection. Her body was smooth and gleaming and I raised a trembling arm to caress it. A shriek of protest coming from the native storeowner stayed my hand. I had not even realized he had left the back room, where he usually stayed. The old man took a hold of the lapels of my jacket and attempted to use his broken English to communicate something to me. I was somewhat distracted by the saliva bubbles flying through his missing teeth, but finally gathered with some difficulty that the statuette was not for sale.

"She is on display, is she not", I asked, shaking him off.

"No sale, no sale," he continued on mumbling. Yellowish foam was erupting on the corners of his cracked lips. He was just inches from my face again. The stench of decay in his breath made my stomach turn; and I took a step back.

"Easy now, old chap," I reasoned with him. "I'll wager you would like to take a few coins home at the end of the day.

"No!" He whimpered, reverting to his incoherent babble, shaking, and looking about ready to go into a seizure. I was beginning to fear that the man was quite mad and maybe not worth all the trouble. Still, the chap was clearly incapable of appreciating Bastet's perfection. He was just clinging to her with the stubbornness of a petulant child. I, on the other hand, had already taken into account the great skill, used by the unknown artist, in carving every little detail. I could think of only a few similar statuettes, all of them in private collections. If pressed, I was perfectly willing to take advantage of my favorable status in Egypt. Ever since the British occupation in 1882, there was close to nothing that could be refused to an Englishman. At the end of the 19th Century, two powers ruled a country of ten million people; The Khedive named Taufig and the British consul. It might be embarrassing to act in that kind of way, but not embarrassing enough to let the statuette go.

I fixed my eyes on those of the store-owner. His turban was tilted on one side. He was gasping for air. I could count every wrinkle on his rugged, brown face. He was shaking his head, silently and once more stating his refusal. His hands were wrapped tightly around the bronze piece. The man was not being reasonable, and he was beginning to surely test my patience.

"Look, we can take matters to the Mixed Courts!" I threatened in a firm voice. "I do not think you realize the unfortunate position you are in," I added. "You will be fined or sent to prison."

He was looking at me with a blank expression on his face.

"She is on display and I must have her," I insisted once more, wondering if I was making any progress at all.

"Why would you take her out, if you did not intend on selling her?" I asked.

My question remained unanswered. He was silent and motionless for a moment, than raised his head as if listening to something. Suddenly, he seemed tired and completely indifferent to the direction our conversation was taking or even my being there.

"We can conclude this unpleasant matter as civilly as possible," I tried to get back to the point. "Or notify the proper authorities. Which shall it be?"

I did not see even a glimmer of coherence on his face. Feeling that the moment called for desperate measures, I pulled out a wad of cash. It was one hundred pound notes that I hadn't exchanged, but rather put aside, only for antique hunting. It was an enormous amount of money that many Egyptians would not earn in a year. With the money in one hand, I took a hold of the statuette with the other. My fingers went over his but he wasn't loosening his grip so I was pulling him and the statuette toward me. The utter desperation on his face had somewhat weakened my hold. My fingers were slipping off when he suddenly let go, and I staggered back. He didn't reach for the cash so I once more held it out to him. His arms hung lifeless on the sides of his body as if no longer attached to his shoulders. I waived a sweaty palm in front of the old man's face then tried to stuff the money into his jacket packet. Betrayed by my trembling fingers I watched helplessly as the notes fell in soft heap to the floor. I attempted to steady my fingers by lasing them firmly around the smooth body of the statuette now completely in my possession. I wanted nothing more than to be out of the dark shop and into my own home. I realized I had been stepping backwards the moment my back touched the rough surface of the door. With my eyes still fixed on the old man's face I reached back for the doorknob. He seemed completely indifferent to either my hasty retreat or the statuette I was holding in my right hand. A powerful wave of endless sadness washed over his face and that was the last thing I saw before getting out of there.

Back on the dusty, humid streets of Alexandria, I quickened my pace, wrapping my jacket around the cat of Bastet trying to conceal her from the prying glances of passersby. I was overwhelmed with the joyous feeling of possessing her. I knew just the place for this perfect new addition to my collection. She belonged on the mahogany mantle of the fireplace in my private study. Although fire was useless in Egypt's climate, a fireplace was something no Englishman could live without. I would then be able to admire my beautiful Bastet, from my comfortable rocking chair, while sipping sherry and enjoying my pipe.

I took the regular route home and decided not to take a cab, but walk since I had left my bicycle at home. It was hard to keep a steady pace, for the narrow streets bubbling with streams of busy people. I had to waive away natives; trying to sell me items I couldn't possibly name and brush away the dirty hands of begging, snotty children, of all ages. The mixed cacophony of knocking, clacking, and yelling soon gave me a headache. Although it was already a late afternoon, the air was sticky with humidity. In a matter of minutes my handkerchief was soaked. I was beginning to regret my decision to walk home for very quickly I was in the midst of too much reality for my taste. Egypt was to me very different than the romantic East described in Arabian Nights or the traveler's journals. In all, it appeared to me as another world. Granted, the landscapes had almost the biblical quality of vast green fields, desert, buffalo, camel, and exotic birds. Yet there was little visual evidence that Egypt had joined the 19th century and the wonders it promised. I discovered a country little changed over time, at once both intriguing and pathetic. Alexandria, where I resided, was its window to the world with a vast native population of Muslims, Jews, and Copts. The European quarter was expansive and consisted not only of French and English families, but also a wide population from the Mediterranean. Greeks, Italians, and Maltese stimulated the commerce as well as the culture of Egypt's most cosmopolitan city. I was employed as an engineer for The Public Works Department. My work was essential in the making of the much-needed straight entrance channel in the sea-port of the city. Since my work was in Alexandria I didn't have to travel on location and endure the sweltering temperatures of Upper Egypt. In my field, experience seemed more important, than one's social status and after my three years in India I had been easily reassigned to Egypt. It was here that I met Mr. Edward Boyle, a British government official and his only daughter Elisabeth. At first meeting them, at the Gentleman's Club, I was subtly, but clearly, made aware of the social discrepancy between a man of plain birth, and a gentleman. Then slowly, and obviously, at Elisabeth's urging, everything changed. As long as I was accompanying the lady or her father I was treated as an equal. I spent many sweltering afternoons and evenings among the country's ruling class- officers, financiers, government officials. All of them, without exception, firmly believed that invading and occupation of another country was a way of redefining Great Britain's imperial policy. I believed in that as well, although maybe not to the extent they did. Any familiarity with the natives, even while at work, was frowned upon. Not that I really needed to make any friends among them. So by the end of my first year in Egypt, I had established a pretty comfortable routine. My social life consisted of seeing Elisabeth, visiting the Club, and once in a while playing tennis. My work hours were short and not particularly demanding, even with a fair amount of paperwork I had to go through each month. I sometimes walked home and visited the antique shops along the way. I discovered the thrill of bargaining, something The East had almost turned into an art form. The most interesting items in my growing collection had cost me little money, as often I was the only one aware of their real value. Granted, the Cat of Basted had cost me considerably more than usual, but she was worth it. I had never before seen anything this beautiful.

Holding the statuette close to my chest, I struggled to erase, from my mind, the desperation I saw on the face of the old storeowner. Pressing him, almost blackmailing him into this transaction, was embarrassing for sure, but not enough so to let her

go to someone else. My steps grew larger, my pace quicker and

my white shirt was soaked with sweat by the time I reached my

house around four o'clock in the afternoon.

CHAPTER TWO

Kasi opened the front door, just as I was reaching for the doorknob, and her familiar, crooked smile was of instant comfort to me. Once again, I congratulated myself on hiring her. She was not only a good housekeeper, but also a trustworthy servant. In the last weeks, she had even become something of a confidant and it was wonderful to have someone, in my household, with experience in domestic matters. Not long ago, with the aid of Sir Edward Boyle, I was reassigned from my dirty, rat infested government lodging to a large, clean house. With my salary now consisting of 850 pounds per annum, I could also afford a cook and a gardener. Kasi was very devoted to me and grateful for the security in her position. Many of the peasants in the country, called fellaheen, were working the fields and living in extreme poverty. Things were not much better for city folks, for they were often in lowly jobs and barely earning enough for their daily bread. More prestigious forms of occupation were held by Europeans-Frenchmen, Greek, German, and of course, Englishmen.

"Tea, Master Richard?" She asked, in her heavily accented English.

"No, thank you." I replied wearily. "But I would love a glass of sherry in the study, please."

I carefully positioned the statuette at the exact center of the mantelpiece and sat heavily in the rocking chair. I was tired, but content. I put a pillow behind my back and prepared to enjoy my evening. The Cat of Bastet was in my house and atop my fireplace; a far more suitable home for her than that dusty old shop, where she was previously residing. Sipping from my glass, I glanced around the pretty room, with its soft Persian carpets, antique German clock and several other beautiful pieces of art. Sometimes I felt that my study looked more like a museum, rather than a regular room. Even my desk was one remarkable piece that had survived in mint condition, long after Napoleon was no longer Emperor. Nevertheless, I enjoyed spending time in this room. It felt good to be surrounded by, and enjoy, all the exquisite items in my now vast collection.

The rest of the house was furnished in the more common, yet comfortable, Victorian style that I had always found very patriotic. Granted, the home, and most of its furnishings belonged to the British Government, but I was to be its primary occupant for the rest of my assignment in Egypt. My future return to England was going to be a glorious one, and a product of very careful planning. Miss Elisabeth Boyle was an essential part of my plans. When we marry, I could go back to having the social and financial status I had always desired, and felt I richly deserved.

My fiancé's chilly disposition, and controlling nature, might have chased away some suitors, but not me. It was still unbelievable to me, that she accepted my proposal, rather than that of someone with better standing in life. I surmised that she most likely wanted to marry before officially being declared an old maid. She also probably expected me to be a complacent and undemanding husband, and I had every intention of being just that. She didn't love me, for she wasn't one of a passionate nature, and I did not have the dashing looks of hero from a fashionable romantic novel. I did not mind, and in fact even welcomed the lack of passion in our connection. After our engagement became official, the relationship reached a good enough level of comfort and security. The state of my personal life suited me very well and I was certain the same was true for Elisabeth.

I topped off my glass with the garnet liquid filling the crystal decanter standing on my desk. I was certainly one to appreciate the finer things in life. The uneasy perspective of our wedding night was far enough in the future. I was confident that I had a fair amount of knowledge in those matters and believed that my future wife would not be completely unhappy with me. Granted, my experience was limited to some of the city's registered prostitutes and had left somewhat of a bitter taste in my mouth. Still, the act itself was not entirely unpleasant, all though the women were not always young and often with shallow complexions. In short not particularly attractive by my standards. Afterwards, I always felt unclean, ridden with guilt, and swore to never resort to a whore again. Unfortunately I never kept that promise. I would wash my hands and privates until raw, but was still unable to resist the urge, when it came. Frankly, I was unable to lead a chaste life and was often succumbing to my most basic instincts. Maybe it would be different when one enters into a lawful liaison with one's wife.

The picture of Elizabeth's pursed lips and pale shoulders I was drawing in my head vanished at a startling sound of something breaking. The door of my study was cracked opened and I was able to see pretty well the windows in the vestibule. The glass on the one on the right had been shattered into hundreds of pieces, now sprinkled on the windowpane. I struggled to stand up, yet after three glasses of sherry and no supper, keeping my balance was a challenge. I caught a glimpse of a shadowy figure, swiftly moving through the door and towards me. I tried to focus my eyes, but my vision was still so fuzzy, and the shape so blurry, that I almost convinced myself I was dreaming. In another moment the figure was in front of me, looking so solid, I knew it was not a figment of my imagination. It was the antique storeowner, the old man whose name I never bothered to find out.

The bloody maniac was holding a pistol in his hand! The shiny silvery-gray piece of metal was pointed right at me! Before I could muster a sound or run for my life, a bullet ricocheted off the wall behind me and hit the mantelpiece on my right. My new statuette was in pieces! At the loud whistle of the second bullet, I managed to cover my ears and doubled over. Before even feeling any pain I saw, with horror, a steady stream of blood spurting out from the bullet wound on my hip. The entire left side of my body quickly grew numb. My legs turned into liquid. I fell on one knee, then the other, trying to hold on to something, but ending up on the floor all the same. The old man's savage, rugged face leaning over me was the last thing I remember before losing consciousness.

Coming to my senses, I looked around, but the room was empty. My attacker must have escaped, obviously coming to terms to what he had done. The possible consequences of his actions would be severe and quite frightening to be sure. I cleared my throat and called for Kasi. My voice was as weak as newborn kitten's. Before trying again, I checked myself remembering her always complaining of bad hearing. She obviously had not heard the shots or she would have rushed to my study already. None of the other servants were allowed to spend the night in the house, so there was no help coming from them either. I forced myself up and shakily walked to the washroom next door, where I kept some first aid supplies. I examined my wound, which seemed to me to be shallow. The bullet had brushed against my hipbone and the bleeding had almost stopped on its own. I winced from the pain which was significant enough to make me light headed. My hands were shaking as I prepared a rough dressing. I was feeling very weak, yet still had to wake Kasi up and have her fetch the police. I also wanted to check the damage done to my study.

That dreadful old man wanted to kill me! Over a piece of bronze! For God's sakes, what was the world coming to? I limped in the direction of the fireplace, holding on to furniture and finally reached the mantelpiece. I did not see the statuette there, or any shards of it on the ground. Still examining the floor, I heard a whimper coming from behind my chair. My heart jumped into my throat. Surely, it was possible that my attacker was laying in wait to finish me off. I moved closer and took a hold of a heavy marble candlestick holder. There was that sound again. It was too delicate to be coming from the old man. I stepped behind the chair and drew the light lower to the floor. My still trembling hand froze in granite like stability. The hot wax began dripping on the bare body beneath me. She was trembling, letting out a moan each time the wax singed her skin and I swiftly drew the candle closer to my chest. Her face was in a shade still and all I could see was a mass of dark hair matted over her shoulders. Her limbs were folded around her; as if she was cold. She resembled a ball of flesh. From the soft bits exposed to me I could surmise with a reasonable certainty that it was a female. I could also tell she was in pain. The gaping bullet wound on her shoulder was gushing massive amounts of blood and even I could tell it was serious. She was not still and quiet anymore.

I positioned the candlestick holder on the ground, far enough so she would not get singed. Next I kneeled down next to her, feeling her warm blood on me, while trying to pick her up. With a sudden burst of strength, she stood shakily on all fours then flopped back on the floor where she thrashed and rolled for what it seemed like an eternity. I couldn't get near enough to help her and my frantic attempts to calm her down came to nothing. At one point I stopped talking, for it looked as if my voice was making her even more frantic. I just tried to take a hold of her and position her into the chair, where I could examine the wound and attempt to stop the bleeding. I was scratched and bitten a number of times, chasing her around, something hard to take on in my present state. I saw her yellow eyes with the frightened look of a trapped animal. During the struggle, through her flipping dark and tangled mane, I thought I saw a pair of small gold earrings. I was concerned that she was losing too much blood, when pain and exhaustion finally defeated her and she suddenly went limp and heavy in my arms. I had to find a place more comfortable than a chair, she was hurt too seriously.

I managed somehow to cross the vestibule; open the door to my bedroom and just before my arms gave in dropped her into bed. She moaned, coming to her senses the moment the pillow touched her shoulders. I leaned my back to the wall. I knew if I sat down I wouldn't be able to stand up again. She was lying motionless now and I limped toward the wardrobe, looking for something I could use to stop the bleeding. I grabbed the first piece of clean linen I could find-a fresh undershirt and pressed it to the wound. It soaked through almost immediately. I used some water I had in a glass on my nightstand to at least rinse the wound. She opened her eyes wide for a second or two, and then closed them wearily. It seemed that the bullet had gone clean through, which I knew to be preferable. I used the sleeves of the shirt in a fashion I hoped to act as a tourniquet and the rest as a dressing. Luckily, the bleeding stopped in a couple of minutes. An hour later, when I changed the bandage, the wound was already beginning to develop a protective crust.

She barely moved for the rest of the evening. By that time, I had decided to deal with Kasi and the police in the morning. I spent a restless night on the floor next to the bed and was checking periodically on my patient. To my surprise, she did not develop fever or any other troublesome symptoms, usually associated with gun shot wounds. Around five o'clock in the morning, she looked to be resting comfortably and I allowed myself to lie back and pause for some reflection. I was still trying to sort out the events of the night. I realized that before me laid the uneasy task of declaring the presence of a young female at my house. Her wound and blatant nudity would add even more weight to the scandal. It soon became apparent to me that calling in the authorities was out of the question. I had no plausible explanation as to how she had come to my home or who she was. She could not have come with the old man since I had seen him breaking in and he was alone. She certainly was not in my study when I had started with my evening. The young woman had appeared after the shooting and after I was wounded. The Cat of Bastet was shattered into pieces, only I couldn't find any of them anywhere. Plenty of strange things have been happening ever since I had laid eyes on the statuette. It was obvious how exclusive the piece have been, since I was almost killed over it. It was so special, that it explained the old man's breaking into my house in hopes to retrieve it. Instead he had destroyed it. Or did he?

As I was drifting into sleep, the mad idea I had been refusing to accept all night, seemed the only possible explanation. Where did she come from? Before falling into dreamless sleep, I already knew the answer. She came from Bastet. She was her daughter.

CHAPTER THREE

I woke up with a start, and the worst possible headache, ready to believe that the whole of last night was only a nightmare. I looked around and found myself still lying on the floor, too exhausted to move and with only a thin throw under my aching body. I could no longer convince my self that the morning was as plain as any other. In fact, it was as far from it as it could possibly be. I raised my self to a sitting position then stood up with caution. I had to get a hold of the night stand to keep myself steady. I felt tired and dizzy but otherwise there was only some numbness in my right leg and almost no pain in my hip. I sat carefully on the ottoman at the foot of the bed and glanced back to check on my patient. I only saw a sizable heap of bed covers. She must have buried herself underneath them to keep warm and was still sleeping.

There was a knock on the door.

"Enter! I said, jumping to fetch my house coat.

Kasi walked through the door, carrying the tea tray. She knew that after I've had a little too much to drink, I preferred having breakfast in my room. I was willing to bet she had with her some wet, hot towels and a couple of aspirins, as well.

"Master Richard! The room!" she gasped, somehow managing to prevent the contents of the tray from splattering on the parquet. I slowly stood up, trying to overcome the stiffness in my body.

"There was a robbery attempt last night." I said carefully. "One of the robbers, a woman was wounded by her accomplice."

I added that I would appreciate her being calm and collected under the circumstances.

"She is recovering in my bed Kasi." I said. "I didn't know what else to do, but to give her a shelter."

Looking quite baffled, Kasi walked to the night table and positioned the tray there. When she turned around to face me, she had almost completely recovered the look of an obliging servant. She did not ask any questions.

"It is better to keep the young lady's presence confidential for the time being, Kasi." I said hurriedly. "I shall soon decide what to do with her. The cook does not usually arrive before noon and by then we can tidy up in the house."

She nodded obediently and I was grateful for her amiability. She began silently picking up the bloody rags and water glasses of the floor. I was waiting impatiently for her to finish and than asked her to help me get changed. She gasped at the blood on my trousers, as I stripped to my undergarments. At this moment, more than ever, I wished I had a butler, instead of a maid. Nonetheless I could not afford to be shy, so I took off every last stitch of clothing and left it on a heap on the floor. Kasi helped me put on fresh undergarments, very discreetly and without looking at my privates. I instructed her to burn all the damaged clothes as soon as possible. With some difficulty I managed to put my house coat on. I tied the belt loosely around my waist and felt ready to face the day. Kasi kneeled down to put my slippers on my feet. I skipped across the room towards the bed, while leaning on her. The covers and pillows were in a messy pile on the bed and I assumed that my patient was still resting after the ordeal she had been trough. I felt on top, trying to find the body shape underneath. I could only find the smoothness of the mattress. I tossed the covers away on the floor and stared in disbelieve at the empty bed. The patient was very obviously no longer there.

"Where, the bloody hell is she?" I uttered, marching about the room and looking in corners and behind curtains. I finally discovered her, doubled over and trembling under the small vanity table at the far side of the room. Some fresh blood had soaked through the dressing and her bruises looked even more pitiful in the daylight. Her dark hair was matted and covering her face, but I could still see one eye, the color of yellow sapphire, alert and following my every movement. I could not get closer then a few feet, without her dashing to another corner, hiding under another piece of furniture, all the while making aggressive, hissing sounds. Droplets of orange urine were trickling down her thighs and onto the wooden floor. Kasi and I took turns in attempting to subdue her but realized quickly that she was much faster than either of us. She did not hesitate to bite and claw her way out either, when she felt cornered. After about half an hour of chasing her about the room, I decided to try a different approach and seduce her with some food and water. I hoped that although she was obviously very frightened, she would be hungry enough to come to me and accept the food. I took the tray with my breakfast, left untouched until now, and put it on the floor just a couple of feet away from the corner she was cowering in. She didn't attempt to retrieve the food and when I tried to push the tray toward her, she growled in warning. She was obviously declaring herself ready to pounce, if I got any closer.

I reasoned that I've had enough abuse in the last 12 hours, to last me a lifetime. So I instructed Kasi to follow me out of the room. I left the door to my bedroom cracked open, hoping that I could observe what she would do next. Maybe if she were alone, she would decide to eat or even go back to bed, something I thought to be quite beneficial for her.

I began my watch, concealed behind a huge potted plant in the vestibule. For a while there was not even the slightest movement inside my bedroom. I was beginning to lose faith in my plan, when I finally saw her crawling out of her corner. She was moving with extreme caution, stopping every few inches, holding her head high. She stopped half way through, to carefully sniff the air. For a moment she froze, her face turned in my direction as if she could sense I was near. Then she continued on her way.

Slowly, she approached the food, delicately sniffing in and around the tray. Next she lowered her head to the ground, still on all fours. She looked almost too lean, her spine easy to trace on her narrow, long back. Her shoulder blades were protruding, her thighs quivering with exhaustion in the pose she had come to. There was nothing exciting about her nakedness she looked a little revolting and very pathetic. I saw her sharp, pink tong going in and out, as she was drinking the sweet cream, still in the pitcher. She didn't even nibble on the bread and butter. She ended up eating couple of morsels of cheese, before returning to her hiding place.

I decided not to wait for any other development pretty soon after I realized there was not much happening in the room. I was feeling famished and headed for my study. There, I enjoyed some early lunch and was able to stretch out and take a much needed nap on the sofa. I must have slept for longer than I had intended because it was time for tea when I awoke.

"Enter." I said in response to the soft knock on the door. I stretched cautiously and stood up. Amazingly, I was feeling no pain anywhere in my body, only some stiffness in my neck and shoulders.

"How is our patient Kasi?" I asked, filling my cup with the strong Ceylon tea, and then adding three lumps of sugar. I needed as much sugar and caffeine I could get.

"I not know Master Richard," my maid answered, handing me a napkin. "I knock on door two times. She dons answer."

I sighed, annoyed, having to deal with this as if I did not have enough on my plate already. Then shrugged my shoulders determined to enjoy my tea.

"Don't worry about it Kasi." I said with flair. "I will check on her before supper."

Sipping my tea, I decided to use the same approach for supper that had worked to some degree for breakfast. My charge was obviously not one that desired to be fussed over, so all I could do was bring her food and water and wish for the best. I was hopeful that at one point she would trust me enough to let me change the dressing on her wound. From what I could tell, there was no fresh blood on it this morning and she seemed to me moving about without pain. How little she had eaten worried me

[28]

though and I decided for supper to change her menu a bit. I was pretty sure there was no raw meat in my kitchen, for my maid went to market each morning and poultry was cooked that same day. I did know however of some smoked beef that I sometimes liked nibbling on. I also, always had a small barrel of salted small fish in the cellar, although Elisabeth had declared long ago that only a "person of mean birth" could enjoy such feast. In the kitchen, I cut the meat and fish in small morsels and after some consideration decided to skip the bread. I wasn't sure weather to choose cream or water for her drink and after some consideration chose the first since she had drunk it at breakfast. I knocked on the bedroom door, than smiled at the uselessness of the act. As if she could actually grasp the meaning or need of good manners.

The door creaked as I opened it and I saw her right the way sleeping under the vanity table, curved in a tiny ball of flesh. In an instant, she was alert and out, this time standing up but in a very awkward manner. She was obviously ready to dart away in whichever direction she felt was safe. My foot wasn't even over the threshold when she ran in lightning speed across the room and scampered under the bed. I was beginning to find her bizarre behavior rather tiresome, nonetheless I pleaded with her in a soft voice to come out. Silence was the only response to my very reasonable pleas. I kneeled down and peaked under the bed. I could only see her eyes, unblinking and following my every movement. I could swear they were glowing in the darkness. I knew better than trying to stick my hand in there and try to pull her out. Such an enterprise would surely end up with considerable pain for me. I had no choice but to let her be.

I left the tray on the floor as I had this morning, then collected the almost untouched breakfast tray and headed out of the room. I hid in the same place in the vestibule as I had before so if I preened my neck just so, I could see a pretty good portion of the room.

This time she came out of hiding almost right the way. Apparently done with straight walking, she was again on all fours. As earlier, she began drinking the cream right out of the pitcher and took her time. She sniffed the beef, but didn't bother with it, selecting and only eating the fish. I used to think that cats ate rather gracefully, so much more delicately than dogs. However, the sight of her eating on her hands and knees was rather unpleasant. I had to force myself to look away from some of the very exposed parts of her anatomy. She looked rather dirty now. The dressing over her wound was gone and there were splotches of dried blood all over her torso. There was nothing more I could do for her tonight under the circumstances. I could only hope that she would decide to spend the night in the warm bed, but I doubted it. Most likely, she would sleep under it or in one of the other hiding places she had discovered today. In any case, I had plenty of other arrangements I needed to make. My study still needed some tiding up and Kasi had to help me move to the guest bedroom. I still had to come up with an acceptable version of the young woman's presence in my bachelor pad. I needed to explain it to the servants at least and thus prevent any malicious gossip.

I locked the bedroom door behind me, cursing myself for not doing this earlier. Luckily she hadn't tried to escape. After supper, I was still contemplating what to do with this unexpected addition to my household. She looked like a young woman, but was acting like a wild animal. It didn't seem that she could speak or understand people talking to her. I couldn't get close to her to attend to her wounds, let alone cover her up for decency sake. It was indecent, the whole affair, and if it seemed that way to me it will look even more so to others. I was hesitant however, surrendering her to the police, even if I was ready to accept the scandal that would surely follow. I had a pretty shrewd idea of the dreadful conditions in Alexandrian insane asylums, to not want to punish her like that. Perhaps, if she is calmer tomorrow as she got better, I could find some way to communicate with her and go from there. The trouble was I had to be gone most of day; I needed to go to work. Granted, I could give Kasi clear instructions as to how to deliver the food to the young creature but otherwise leave her alone. I could check on my patient myself in the morning and again upon my return. I slept soundly, despite the unfamiliar new bedroom and the many disruptive thoughts going through my head.

CHAPTER FOUR

I awoke Monday morning, not very rested, but ready to begin my week in fighting spirits. I washed and got dressed quickly and then headed for the dining room to have breakfast. I wasn't feeling very hungry, but forced myself to eat a piece of toast and some eggs. I was too tired from the last two, somewhat traumatic days, to afford to miss out on the most important meal of the day. I also drank pretty quickly two cups of strong black tea with lots of sugar. That could get me going most mornings. As for today I had to wait and see. I needed to look as if nothing out of the ordinary had happened to me and prevent any unhealthy curiosity at work. I was feeling a little weak though. Luckily, the wound on my hip looked not to be infected and did not hurt anymore. All I had to do was conquer my exhaustion and keep up with appearances this week. The rest just had to fall into place.

I prepared a plate of salted fish for my uninvited guest's breakfast and headed for my old bedroom. Even while on the way I could feel the food doing its beneficial work. I felt that I had regained almost all of my old strength. I was praying to find my patient more civil this morning than she was yesterday. I did not bother knocking this time, what would the point be of that particular exercise? I pressed en ear on the door and my patient was either sleeping, or the wood was too solid, because I did not hear anything. As my foot went over the threshold, I almost chocked on a horrible stench. The smell of excrements was so overpowering, that I immediately started breathing through my mouth.

"Dear Jesus!" I gasped, walking in and by this point well aware that she had…relived herself. I covered my nose and mouth with a clean handkerchief, trying to locate the source of the vile odor. Apparently, after she had finished her meal last night, she needed a place to use and I was a fool for assuming that it would be the proper one. There was of course, a chamber pot underneath the bed and she must have seen it, while hiding under it so many times. Obviously, she had not given it enough thought to actually use it. Instead, she had chosen the beautiful flowerpot, in which Kasi had just recently planted English roses! Their pleasant scent was completely overpowered now by the stench of waste. How did she reach the pot, was mystery to me, for it was standing high on the wide windowsill. For a moment, I saw the hilarious picture of her perched on the sill, going at it. Only, I was too nauseated to laugh.

"That bloody woman!" I murmured, backing slowly out of the room.

I was too astonished to spend any time in looking for the woman. She was probably hiding, feeling guilty for the mess she had made of my bedroom. I could see enough of the bed and the rest of the furniture to barely recognize it. I could wager I saw some nail scratch marks on the night table. As soon as she is somewhat recovered, I wanted to be rid of her for good. My stomach was queasy and I was too frustrated to abandon the breakfast I had prepared with much care, anywhere in the room. God only knows, what else that little animal had done on every available surface in there. I didn't even bother to find out how she had spent the night. It would not matter even if I had. I couldn't get closer than couple of feet, without her attacking me or running away. I hadn't seen her in the open in the room and I assumed that she was in concealed, as usual. By the time I went back to the kitchen, I was able to somewhat collect myself. I briskly informed Kasi, that from now on she would be responsible for the complete care of the young woman, and that included feeding her and cleaning after her.

"I desire, to have as little to do with her as possible," I declared, then headed to my room. I felt compelled to once again change my clothes and get ready for work. I was already late.

It seemed, as if the horrible stench of excrements, stayed lingering on my hair, skin, and I could smell it even after washing thoroughly. I was in no mood to use my bicycle that morning, which could have helped to air out the vile odor. Instead I decided to catch a coach. There were plenty of those, stationed on almost every corner at the European quarter and it only cost a few piasters to go anywhere. As usual, I did not speak to the coachmen and chose to look at his back and sloppy turban, instead of his face. I arrived at Public Works Department, determined to make the best of the upcoming week.

The next few days, I performed my duties with a devotion and enthusiasm I hadn't felt since the beginning of my assignment in Egypt. During the evenings while at home, I kept mostly to my study, resuming my usual activities such as reading historical books or cataloguing properly the items of my collection. I still had not exactly come to grips with what had happened over the weekend. I knew I had to quickly decide what to do with the unexpected addition to my household. I just kept postponing the making of that decision in the hope, that the problem would somehow resolve itself. The only time, on Friday when I decided to go and visit the young woman, she didn't behave in a manner anymore civilized than before. For half an hour, she kept on running away and hiding from me, until I left in frustrated huff. Surprisingly, I have noticed on that same visit that Kasi's, presence was being tolerated, even enjoyed. The young woman ran from me straight to the arms of my maid, as if looking for protection. Then, Kasi would hold her tight, as if trying to shield her from all the rest of the world. My maid seemed to enjoy caring for the creature and was spending hours in the bedroom, now kept (I didn't wish to know how) completely fresh and clean. She did not look the least disgusted, in having to take care of the young women's most basic needs.

As another week rolled by, Kasi began to express an often growing empathy for our roommate. She repeatedly harped on the need of a name for the young woman, so we could address her properly. She insisted that we should keep talking to her, with the hope that she would learn some words and even speak back to us in complete sentences some day.

"I know she could understand me," she said, certainly being optimistic.

I did not share her enthusiasm, yet abandoning my supposed indifference for a moment, I suggested, "Her name will be Ciara. It is an Old Irish name meaning "black". I paused, suddenly wandering why I chose that particular name.

"It will match the color of her hair," I decided, then drifted back in thought again, remembering the face of my beloved grandmother. She carried that same name and was the only person in my childhood, which expressed kindness and love to me. My Nanna possessed the fresh, rosy complexion that Irish women are so proud of. Soft, feathery wings of white hair were framing her lovely face. Her eyes were as blue as the sky and just as clear. She had a gift for singing and knew many fascinating tales of bravery and strength. Oh, how I loved sitting in her lap and listening to her stories. In them, there was always a happy ending and the characters were courageous heroes, never afraid of anything. While she was still alive, my mother treated me with some civility. That all changed, with my grandmother's passing. My mother never spoke to me again, without contempt. I was the last, viable link to a dead husband she truly detested while he was alive. Things got even worse, after she remarried. She would speak to me only rarely and always without actually looking at me, but rather through me, as if I was made out of air.

"Get out of that room child, I want to be in it," was her usual and often only address to me for that day. She was strongly opposed to my stepfather's desire to pay for my schooling; for she was certain that I would be totally unable of accomplishing anything of worth in my life. In the end, I was able to go to Cambridge, finding one way, or another, to earn my tuition money. I paid, without a doubt, a high price for my education. Sometimes I still would have nightmares and relive the things my stepfather used to do to me. Then I would lie awake for hours, unable to pull myself out of the black hole, I had fallen into so many years ago.

But that is another story altogether and one I do not wish to remember.

Yes. Ciara was a very special name and it strangely suited the young creature. When I gave it to her it was simply a name. And it brought the sweet memory of my dear grandmother back to me. "Black" was nothing else, but describing the young woman's rich hair color. It was much later that I realized, with startling clarity, that it also held a clue to explaining the supernatural way The Daughter of Bastet came into my life. It also held a deep meaning of how irreversibly, and forever, Ciara was going to change it. And that she did, without even trying and without the powers I never knew she possessed, until the very end of our tale together.

CHAPTER FIVE

Days were slowly turning into weeks and I began to feel renewed, yet unexpected interest in Ciara. It began gradually, with visiting her once in a while, but she was getting to be so interesting that I began spending more and more time with her. Soon, and with Kasi's encouragement, I was spending every free afternoon with Ciara. Teaching her even the smallest things was a surprising source of a complete and unadulterated delight. I could finally understand the excitement of an artist laying his first paint stroke on the bare canvass or the joy of a writer, putting his first paragraph on a blank sheet of paper. I had heard of that kind of excitement before, but that was the first time, in my life, I could truly relate to it. My mission was more exciting than that, my work more empowering and my efforts more rewarding. I had the rare opportunity of turning a wild creature into a human being and the chance of molding her into the young woman she was (I was certain by that time) destined to be. I didn't expect to be capable of such a patience, affection and strength. Every time we reached another milestone in her development, I felt happier and more fulfilled.

At first, it was difficult for Ciara to feel safe with me even being in the same room with her. Days passed by, before she would let me get near her or touch her, without pulling away with distrust and fear. Little by little, she began getting used to her surroundings, to Kasi and me, to all the strange things and unfamiliar smells around her. One of the things I liked best was brushing her long hair in the mornings. The first time I did it, it took almost an hour to smooth out all the tangles and knots in it. Every couple of minutes she would pull away and lazily bite on the brush. The end result was worth it though. She looked very decent, with her hair neatly set and her face freshly washed. Soon, she was comfortable enough to tolerate and even enjoy that daily routine. She especially liked someone else to brush her hair for she would be purring to express her delight and contentment. Once in a while, she would attempt to arrange her hair herself and would do a pretty good job of it. Still, she obviously preferred for someone else to be pampering her and Kasi and I were always up to the task.

To have Ciara take a bath was another matter entirely. It was not calm and pleasant. Ciara was so terrified of the water in the tub that no coaxing could make her go in it. It did not make any difference how hard I tried to convince her it was safe. She would become frantic as soon as we entered the washroom and nothing could make her believe that taking a bath was pleasant and beneficial. Some days I felt so frustrated that I even considered dunking her in the tub myself and holding her down there. Then I remembered how strong and obstinate she could be. I had just earned her trust I certainly did not want to lose it again. Besides, she did seem to be instinctively and truly frightened by the water, so forcing her to go in it was obviously a bad idea. So, for the time being, Kasi accepted yet another responsibility. She was supposed to give her a sponge bath every evening and wash her hair with head over the tub once a week. That way everybody was happy and my patient remained clean.

I was truly pleased, when finally all of Ciara's scrapes and bruises healed properly. That presented another problem though. Now, that she was healthy, I was beginning to feel quite uneasy always seeing her in the nude. Never mind that she seemed completely unaware of the very indecent state she was in. I felt hard pressed to do something about it and do so quickly. Kasi was constantly commenting about the impropriety of a bachelor, sharing the same house with a nude woman. Of course, putting even the simplest piece of clothing on our young charge seemed difficult, if not impossible. She would claw at the shirt or bite on the stockings with such a consistency that soon she would tear them to pieces.

I had instructed Kasi to buy lady's undergarments of the finest linen, yet I could see that Ciara found them so restraining that she was persisting in taking them off. Finally, I decided instead of putting an entire outfit on her, to start slowly with culottes or a shirt and each week to add another item of clothing. That way she would have seven days to get used to each additional piece and hopefully make a successful transition to being fully dressed.

The first time I put a loose nightshirt on her, she tore it again to pieces in a matter of minutes. I wasn't willing to give up that easily so Kasi and I proceeded with our plan. We dressed her in another shirt that very same evening. This time, she kept it on for twenty minutes and wiggled out of it without tearing it up. We persisted on putting it back on over and over again. It took a few tries but by the time we bid her goodnight at eleven o'clock, Ciara was ready to go to sleep and with a nightshirt on. This was a complete victory as far as I was concerned. For the six nights afterwards, she became gradually accustomed to wearing it to bed, so we decided to move on to lady's culottes. Ciara tired of taking them of in mere few days and in a couple of weeks she was walking around in her undergarments. After that we moved on to dresses and stockings. Soon, she was able to get dressed all by herself. She would even participate in choosing her own outfit for the day. Wearing shoes still proved challenging for her and she was constantly taking them off. I was hopeful though that with the passing of time she would get use to wearing them all the time. Wisely, and at Kasi's suggestion, I had decided not to try to put Ciara into a corset, certain that she would find it to too constraining. Besides, her waist was so tiny that dresses looked completely streamlined on her, as if she was wearing one.

I was very proud to see her looking so presentable, so fast. I planned on ordering her entire wardrobe from a very reputable dressmaker in town. All items were to be made out of soft fabrics and happy, vivid colors. I was determined not to allow in her wardrobe any of the pastels that were in fashion at the moment. Ciara would certainly look stunning in vibrant yellows, blues, and reds.

Ciara was beginning to talk with amazing speed and was quickly becoming quite the little conversationalist. Her vocabulary was still poor, but she was eager to learn more and was always asking questions. In the mornings, before my going to work, we would have breakfast together and I would always try to teach her few new words. If time permitted, I would come home for lunch and we would again have a meal together and continue, for a bit, our morning lessons. Sometimes she would have difficulty building a sentence or to answer a question herself. Still she was beginning to reveal the understanding of an adult of certain subjects. It was almost as if she had known how to speak long ago and now she was simply relearning it. Little by little, Ciara began using a knife and a fork as well, but was handling them awkwardly, the way a young child does. With considerable difficulty, I was able to convince her to have her meat cooked, but for a while nothing in the world could make her drink anything other than milk or water. Once, when I held a glass of sherry to her nose so she can smell it, she started sneezing and coughing violently. The drink's potent vapors were obviously too strong and very objectionable to her. After that incident, she never showed any interest in a drink with any amount of alcohol in it. She eventually got used to drinking tea though, especially with lots of sugar. She was hilarious, holding a porcelain teacup to her lips, not sipping, but slurping its content, which she preferred, lukewarm, never hot. Needless to say, fish was still her favorite treat and she quickly discovered the most effective way to beg for it. It was impossible to refuse her anything, when she would put her small paw on my lap, eyes unblinking.

"Pleeease, Rrichard," She would say, with eyes fixed on the plate. "Ciara wants." That was enough.

She knew, very early on, that with me she did not need to say much to be effective. It was thrilling to see her trying to pronounce certain words. She tended to drag out the "a" and "e' and sometimes understanding her was a challenge. But her memory appeared capable of maintaining quite a decent vocabulary. I was ready to melt in delight the day she said my name for the first time. From her mouth, it sounded almost like a growl, with a long, hard "R" but it was the best, most special gift; anyone has ever given me. Usually, after dinner I would tuck her in bed, gently caressing her face and soft hair, until she would start purring. I could tell she was feeling so warm and safe. By the time I would give her a good night kiss, she would be sleeping, but somehow still very aware of every movement and sound in the room. The ancient predatory instincts in her nature, present in the beginning, did not dissolve completely in her rapid progress. I would often see her standing almost completely motionless and only with the swift movement of her head, following the flight of a bird or the flapper of a butterfly. Not even insects could escape a tragic fate, once she had it in her mind to track them down and squish them between her delicate paws. The amazing speed of her movements, the clarity of her direction, and the concentration with which she acted, were absolutely fascinating to observe. She was stronger and quicker, than any creature I have ever seen going after its' pray.

Ciara's affections were subtle to express and slow to be earned and therefore even more precious to me. I could pride myself of winning her trust and attachment for whenever I walked into the room she would run to me with greeting on her lips and an awkward hug. It was more like she would rub her cheek against my jacket while holding at the lapels of my jacket. I felt happier and more content than ever before and was looking forward to our time together each and every day.

With her physical health so much improved and her curiosity awakened Ciara became a restless little being. I would have enjoyed her energy and playfulness, if not for the fact that still no one, other than Kasi and me knew of her residing at my home. A little more than a month had passed since she came to me, and for the time being, we were successful at keeping her presence a secret. It did take quite en effort on our part and now she was making matters even more difficult. I guessed I could let her explore the house, so long as she stayed away from the windows. However, that was not enough for her anymore. The time had come when Ciara felt ready to go out.

She wanted to play in the garden or explore the streets and didn't seem to understand my fear of her being seen. It was heartbreaking to see her sleep so much, an easy way for many animals to escape their boredom. I knew I couldn't keep her behind closed doors forever, for it was a cruel restriction to impose on such a lively creature. For some time, I have been searching for a way of making her stay with me legitimate and accepted to everyone. I have been toying with the idea of presenting Ciara as a relative of some sort. She could be a cousin or a niece, some sort of kin, to whose fate I couldn't possibly be indifferent. I was somewhat concerned about people remarking on the darker color of her skin and brunette hair, so opposite of mine. People might gossip about such a girl, having an uncle with a freckled skin and blonde hair. Then again, society might not even consider that odd. It was only minor details in one's physical appearance.

The true obstacles, to her coming out, remained her odd speech and almost complete ignorance of social boundaries. The legend of a poor niece with troubled development could play out successfully only with the help of a powerful ally. I needed a clever helper too, which can make Ciara's presence known in our circles, while preventing gossip. Elisabeth seemed the perfect candidate for the mission, for she answered all the requirements. My fiancée possessed an excellent social status and plenty of experience in dealing with difficult situations. I could also count on her wanting to protect my reputation and family name, since she still wished to marry me someday. I cursed myself for calling on her only once in the past two months. What was worse, I was guilty of barely even thinking of her in that period of time. I had sent her couple of letters, blaming loads of work and a recent ailment for my inability to see her. But knowing Elisabeth as well as I did, I could suppose with reasonable certainty that she would be displeased with me. I did not think that she would do something as distasteful as make a scene or break our engagement. Yet she might be hesitant to help me in my endeavor. I was already convinced that her good will was exactly what I needed to carry out my plan and I just had to earn it all over again. I scribbled out a short note to Elisabeth, inviting her for tea the coming Saturday afternoon.

I was going to behave in very attentive and caring manner and then serve her with some sob story about a poor girl, who had no one else, but me in the whole world. Elisabeth was one, always very concerned with family obligations and I was hoping to move her with empathy for the poor orphan. Or at least make her feel flattered that her help was so urgently needed. I was ready to beg her forgiveness for ignoring my duties to her and was optimistic that she would accept my apologies. I would take my fiancée to see Ciara, only after feeling reasonably certain, that things are settled in the most favorable way and she is willing to help me. My girl would look as presentable as possible; I would make sure of that. I must also talk to her, so she would be prepared to accept visitors. I had to make sure, that Ciara would be at ease around a stranger, for thus far she was used to be around Kasi and myself only. It was very fortunate that Elisabeth was a lady, too accomplished to voice any stringent disapproval for my behavior, or the situation.

I awaited the arrival of Saturday, with some anxiety. Still, I was much too busy in preparation for Elisabeth's visit to worry too much. I was quite sure, that if I played my cards right, I would actually win this game. Granted, the stakes were high, because if I lost, I would lose Ciara as well. On the other hand, if I won we could stay together and I could keep on being happy and fulfilled in the role of her father, or in our case "her uncle".

CHAPTER SIX

I tried to remain calm and focused that Saturday afternoon, but shortly before teatime I was beginning to feel quite frantic. The confidence I had had in my plan, just few days prior, had turned into quiet desperation. It was very frightening, the thought of trusting Elizabeth and putting everything out in the open. I was in a very vulnerable position. If she refused to help me or was suspicious in any way, nothing could save me from intense scrutiny and even disgrace. Everything I had done to establish myself in society would have been in vain. For yet another time, I berated myself for being careless with my fiancée and taking her for granted. I was beginning to fear that my apologies would be too little, too late. She might even do the unthinkable and dissolve our engagement. She had sent me a note back that she was coming for tea after all and I struggled to see that as a good sign.

The sound of the doorbell catapulted me from my chair and I rushed to the door, feeling my heart pounding in my chest.

Elisabeth was standing at the door alone and for a moment I did not know how to react in the absence of a chaperone.

"Elisabeth, my dear," I collected myself, holding the door opened for her. "It is a delight to see you. Please come in."

She walked into the vestibule and then headed for the dining room in her usual controlled manner and without waiting to see if I was following. Every gesture of hers was measured and every movement had a meaning. She turned around and held out her hand, but I pulled her closer and kissed her on the cheek. The surprise in her eyes slowly vanished as she turned away. She sat on the sofa, her back completely straight and her legs, crossed at the ankles. I took this as an opportunity to sit down next to her and poured the strong, aromatic liquid in her cup. She didn't take off her hat and for a time we were quietly sipping our tea, interrupted only by the delicate clink of a spoon twirling in a porcelain cup.

"My dear," I finally got enough courage to speak. "Please forgive my carelessness. I have been so busy at work, that I have ignored my obligations to you."

Elisabeth kept her head down and the plumes of her hat were somewhat overshadowing her face. I could not read her expression, as I hinted for troubles at home as well and how overwhelmed I have been.

"Lately, I have had the added responsibility to care for my niece," I ventured to say. "She is an unfortunate girl!" I sighed, still unable to guess as to Elisabeth's feelings."

"Her parents passed away, not even two months ago, and I took her in. She had no other place to go." Sill not looking at Elisabeth I added, "Her mind is one of a child and the doctors can not help her."

"How old is she?" Elisabeth's question startled me.

"Why, I don't know exactly," I said hurriedly. "I believe she is one and twenty this summer," I added in more collected manner. "I simply don't know what to do with her. I need your advice on how to best deal with her!"

Still not daring to look at her face, I reached out and took her small hands in mine. She didn't attempt to pull them out. Instead, she left them limp and frigid in my eager grasp.

"I need your help," I said finally looking up.

During my short tirade, Elisabeth had remained silent with the exception of that one question. The expression on her face was now that of polite interest. My heart was racing, as I scooted closer, still holding her hands. I rubbed them gently, wanting to warm them up. She was observing me carefully and an odd feeling of discomfort made me look away.

"I was going out of my mind!" I said trying to break the silence. "You must forgive me and give me a chance to make it up to you! You must!"

Her eyes searched mine for a proof of my sincerity, and then she slowly rose up and nodded. "Take me to your niece, Richard, "she said. "Before I promise anything, I wish to see her."

My knees were trembling, as we headed to the bedroom, side by side. Elisabeth took me by the crook of the arm and I pressed her hand to the side of my body. Once again, I was beginning to feel hopeful for the way everything would turn out. Granted, my fiancé wasn't making any promises but her future remained intertwined with mine. Besides, I was reasonably certain that she would like Ciara. All of my "niece's" odd behavior could be explained away with lack of sturdy mental capacity. My girl had a way of getting under your skin and Elisabeth would be unable to resist her.

Ciara ran to me as soon as I opened the door, which was her usual way of greeting me. She stopped abruptly, seeing me holding the door opened for Elisabeth. Ciara's attention was instantly focused on the strange woman, entering the room. She glowered at Elisabeth, while sniffing the air, her little nose crinkled and pink at the tip. I called her over, in a low and beguiling voice. She paid no heed and suddenly I remembered the early days of her arrival.

"Ciara, come to me," I called again. "I want you to meet someone very special."

"Come on," I repeated, with some urgency now. "Be a good girl and say hello."

Finally my "niece" seemed to have heard me. She took a roundabout way, getting to me, obviously trying to avoid walking near Elisabeth. Ciara used a few clumsy words to express her content for seeing me, but did not hug me. And she did not look content. She seemed distracted and her eyes were following every movement of my fiancée's.

"How do you do, my dear," Elisabeth said, taking a few steps towards Ciara. She froze, on her face the expression of cold distrust and fear. Disregarding this, Elisabeth walked closer, whispering words of comfort and holding out her hand, with a silk purse dangling on the wrist. A moment later she yelped in pain. The whole incident happened so quickly, I had no time to react. My fiancée was holding her scratched; bleeding arm with a look of complete bewilderment in her eyes. Ciara had retreated in a corner and was standing there, with back straight against the wall. Her gaze remained focused on the older woman. Her entire demeanor, made it clear she was determined to attack again at the slightest provocation.

The so anticipated visit had ended abruptly, badly, and I locked the bedroom door, leaving the little aggressor to her own means.

Elisabeth was shaken up and I attended to her scratches with care, grateful for the delay of her decision, no longer certain of its favorable outcome. I remembered how frustrated I had been at first, with Ciara's savage behavior. Why should my fiancé feel any different?

"Richard, your niece is completely….wild." She said, her voice trembling. "You can't take her to the places we go to and her manners have much to be desired."

She put her hand on my shoulder and added, "You can't abandon her, I know." Her face was grave. "People would talk, which would be devastating to our reputations."

She paused, thinking. "There shall be a way to introduce her to society here, making her poor development known of course," she added.

"Thank you, my dear," I replied, feeling immense relief.

"Once we are back in England," Elisabeth said looking me straight in the eye "she must go to a place, where she could be properly cared for."

I looked at her pleadingly, without saying a word.

"We cannot possibly keep her, when we are in London," she reasoned with me. "You realize that I hope?"

"I do, I was just thinking…" I mumbled. "We shall choose a proper way for her coming out," I added. "As for the rest…there will be plenty of time to decide which way to go."

"She can stay with you for the time being," Elisabeth said as if indulging a child.

She gently reminded me that although it is difficult to put a relative in a home, it is usually the best solution for all concerned. She expressed her understanding for my having second thoughts on the subject and her willingness to give me enough time to get used to the idea.

Wishing to change the subject, Elisabeth then suggested an outdoor garden party for Ciara's coming out. She considered it the perfect way to introduce my "niece" to part of the European society in Alexandria. I was to invite a few government officials, their families, and hope that the familiar surroundings of my home would help her to behave well among strangers. Elisabeth assured me that once she was accepted among them, she would be so anywhere else in town.

"All you have to do now my dear is to prepare her for the challenge," Elisabeth added. I could tell that she considered this easier said than done and so did I.

I called a cab for her and sent her home, once again declaring my undying devotion to her. The door hadn't closed behind her and I was already planning, as how to best tackle the next task at hand. First, I had to prepare Ciara and then my household for the first Garden Party ever held on the premises. I have never hosted one before, but I knew enough about what needed to be served and the sort of people to invite. The harder part still, was making sure that my "niece's" behavior would be acceptable to the guests. I could help her become more confident by letting her explore the garden and meet my other servants. Hopefully, she wouldn't act as dreadfully with them as she just had with Elisabeth. After the coming out party, I can begin taking Ciara on short walks around the neighborhood. Gradually, she could start meeting some of my colleagues and friends. I had decided to give myself two weeks to prepare everything and I was hoping that would be enough of a time frame for the Party to be a success.

CHAPTER SEVEN

I allowed Ciara to go out to the garden the very next morning, after Elisabeth's visit. At first she was hesitant to abandon her safe area at the front door. She stood there for a while, sniffing the air, turning her head to look at the sky and the clouds. She took her time taking in everything around her. She was absorbing all the new and wonderfully amazing smells and sounds, with every fiber of her body. As if for the first time in my life, I breathed in the flowery scent of the warm air and felt the softness of the grass, beneath my feet. For a while we both were just enjoying the beautiful, sunny day. Then she took off running. She circled around every bush, rushed through every path that was winding through the orchards. She stopped once to rub her little nose on my face, in expression of her gratitude, and then started hoping around again. Her energy seemed never ending. Her long, dark hair was wind blown and tousled and I saw the pure joy of life in the expression on her face. It must have been amazing for her to run free, after the strict confinement of the house. The garden was not big, but she was very excited to explore it every inch of it. She looked completely fascinated by the fig and orange trees and the tiny pond, positioned among them. That morning, she sat there for hours, following with her eyes the swimming fishes. Once in a while she would catch one and would observe with great concentration its flapping movement in her hand. I made Ciara put the fish back in the pond, out of principal, yet I felt as if I was taking a wonderful toy away from her. Needless to say, we had lunch under the trees that day, discreetly observed by servants and some of our neighbors.

For the next few days, my girl remained interested and quite content, to stay in the garden. Soon, there was not even a square foot of ground that was left undiscovered. That newfound freedom of movement seemed to have positive influence on her mindset, as well as her physical state. She quickly developed a rosy, healthy color on her cheeks; her eyes sparkled with life and happiness. In the next two weeks, I saw her spirit awaken. She was no longer the primitive, simple creature I had once known. She was curious about everything around her and was asking a hundred questions a day.

"How does grass grow? Why is the sky blue? Do trees talk?" That was to name just a few. I was amazed though with the originality and depth of her thinking. How interesting her questions must have been if I did not even know how to answer some of them.

In the mean time, I was working every day on improving her manners. She was adhering with less rebellion, and more understanding, to proper customs and boundaries. I joked sometimes that soon Ciara could go to an audience with Queen Victoria and not embarrass us. With her behavior improved, there was not much else to ask for. Her perfect beauty was never in question, for she was fascinating to look at.

She possessed natural grace as well, which combined with her obvious innocence made her completely irresistible, even if her manners were not yet beyond reproach. Everyone in my household had quickly come to adore her and spoiled her terribly. The cook, named Sámi, made every effort to cook food that she would like. He always kept a fresh supply of salted fish, although her diet was a lot more varied of late. The gardener, named Midi, had fresh flowers for her room each morning and enjoyed showing her how to plant perennials. Kasi was spending so much time with Ciara, that she often neglected her other duties. They all wanted her love, which she gave them but always in small doses. She was my girl, though. I was flattered to see her being most affectionate to me. With me, Ciara was very loving and seemed to trust me implicitly. She would always listen to me with attention and obedience I found delightful. My hope that the two women in my life would begin to like each other, was apparently not going to be justified. The one time, when Elisabeth and her father came to dinner, Ciara refused to leave her room, but I wasn't protesting. Keeping the two of them separate, seemed a good strategy to me. As far as Elisabeth was concerned, I made sure to have lunch with her at the Club or at home once a week. I was determined to never again make the mistake of being careless or take her for granted.

Ciara's coming out Garden Party, happened on a Sunday afternoon that arrived with the most glorious sunshine. I had picked out a cream colored dress for her to wear, that enhanced the golden tones of her skin and the warm darkness of her hair. It also underlined her slender figure and long limbs. Ciara was standing, next to Elisabeth and me, at the front porch, welcoming the visitors. The first hour of the affair flew by with pleasant activities and without any unsightly accidents. My girl looked and behaved as a perfect young lady. My guests seemed very agreeable to the refreshments being served. In fact many of them seemed to already have too much to eat and drink. By word of mouth, almost everyone seemed to know of my "niece" already and very few questions were addressed to me. Those I answered as calmly and comprehensively as possible. They were mostly about Ciara's background or her disability anyway. It was not difficult to give people somewhat limited information, with the excuse of the whole thing being a family affair.

I was so proud of my "niece". She was walking about the garden, behaving in a completely acceptable manner. Granted, she acted livelier and laughed louder than most of the other girls her age. Nonetheless, most of the guests couldn't help but smile back at her. Even my future father in law, Sir Edward Boyle, usually extremely reserved, seemed to find her charming. I saw Ciara chatting with many of the guests and no one seemed to mind her oddly built sentences or somewhat sudden, jerky movements.

I had let my guard down for a moment and my many obligations as a host prevented me from monitoring her behavior at all times. When I finally had an opportunity to look for her, she was nowhere to be seen. I looked at some of her favorite spots in the garden and searched among some of the guests she had talked to. Finally, I approached a group of ladies, standing in a circle whispering and staring at something. My worst fears were soon to be confirmed. There was Ciara, no longer wearing hat or shoes, standing completely motionless, as if she wasn't even breathing. The power of her glare was so intense that I instinctively looked up at the same direction. She certainly was on a watch for something in the bushes, but what? Finally, I saw her target. It was a small bird, in plain gray feathers, chirping a cheerful tune. Ciara's sudden, powerful leap made everyone gasp in astonishment, as I yelled at her to stop. It was too late! She caught and twisted the neck of the tiny creature between her long, elegant fingers as swiftly and as calmly, as if she was performing a lot more traditional task. Like knitting or embroidery or any other more traditional lady's pastime. Her next action was also decidedly unfeminine. With steady hands, she inserted the limp body of her victim between her jaws. A lonely feather remained stuck on her chin as she began to look for somewhere safe to escape with her pray.

"Let go of it! Right the way!" I commanded, my voice trembling with disgust and frustration. She looked at me, blinked then slowly, hesitantly walked towards me. When she was no more than a foot away, she dropped the disheveled bundle at my feet. I forced myself to lean over and remove what was left of the bird, from the ground, then wrapped it carefully in my handkerchief. People around us were whispering and the group was expanding and getting more scandalized by the minute. I considered everything lost, when I saw my savior-Elisabeth speaking quietly to some of the guests. She moved from one group to another, all the while talking, without a pause. She was composed and confident and whatever her explanation of Ciara's bizarre behavior was, people deemed it acceptable. It wasn't long before some of the ladies expressed their empathy for the "poor little thing" and their admiration of my noble character in caring for my unfortunate niece. I could barely hear them or comprehend their words. The party was over for my "niece". I grabbed her arm and dragged her to her bedroom, instructing her to wash her face and hands immediately, to scrub them clean. The disturbing vision of the savage young predator, didn't give me a rest for the remainder of the day.

Upon my return to the garden, I saw that Elisabeth had already ordered it to be gorgeously lit from every possible angle by the multicolored paper lamps. She assured me, that everyone was entirely understanding of my domestic situation. Nevertheless, I could hardly wait for the evening to be over. It was no longer fun for me. I was blind to the beauty of my place in the warm evening and deaf to the joyful chatter of my guests. Around ten o'clock the time finally came for my visitors to say good bye. I could hardly stand the happy, drunk crowd any longer. Elisabeth stayed with me, until every single guest had left and before sending her home, I kissed her hand. I hoped I was able to tell her how grateful I was for her help.

"Without you, I would be nothing, my dear," I said wearily, but with conviction.

She seemed to completely agree with that assessment.

That night, I retired to my bedroom early and without kissing Ciara goodnight. My anger abated somewhat at the thought that for the time being her stay at my home was known and approved of. I could enjoy spending time with both-Ciara and Elisabeth, without worrying about scandalizing anyone or invoking any unpleasant gossip.

CHAPTER EIGHT

Time was flying by and I was determined to maintain at least an appearance of ordinary days. But my life could not have been more different.

On the afternoons, I would sometimes stop for a drink and a conversation at the Club, but often found the experience rather dull. It is not that we talked only scandal at the Club, but very little useful business was done there. I found myself cutting those visits short and going home. I made sure on seeing Elisabeth at least once a week, grateful for her help and now wishing to feel closer to her. The time we spent together was pleasant enough and our conversations were always clever and entertaining. Still, sometimes I wished that she was not quite as cool and in control as she was. It would have been nice for her to demonstrate her affection in ways, better suited for a fiancée. I would have enjoyed it, if once in while we held hands or kissed. I was pretty sure that no one would have found that inappropriate. We were engaged to be married, after all.

I kept telling myself that her obvious distaste of any physical intimacy was a sign of her good breading. I struggled to conceal my disappointment. Anyway, it was rather unwise to be disappointed now, for I knew what I was in for, the moment Elisabeth and I met. Our relationship was not one possessed by the fiery passion, described in romantic novels. Instead it was a comfortable and mutually beneficial partnership. I didn't need the inconvenient emotion called love to make me happy. I was willing to make the best of our relationship, such as it was. Yet some part of me, kept on hoping that one day we would share more and be closer.

For the time being, Elisabeth was perfectly willing to hear about work and support me in my career. She could talk endlessly as to how we were going to furnish our home or the style of the coach we were going to own. She seemed very interested in what I had to say, when it came to our future together. Yet, she rarely wanted to hear anything about my innermost thoughts, my hopes and dreams. She was especially indifferent when it came to discussing Ciara. I knew the two of them had started on the wrong foot, but I wished that I could tell my fiancée, how special the young girl was to me. Or describe to her, how proud I was of her beauty and her grace. My girl was making amazing progress in her development each and every day. Who could I share this with, but the person that is supposed to be closest to me? But Elisabeth made it perfectly clear that anything, having to do with my "niece", was not an agreeable topic of conversation.

In my relationship with Ciara I could not ask for anything more. She was emotionally and physically warm and affectionate to me. The time spent with her was the most exiting in my day. I could hardly wait to finish work, so I could get home. The unpleasant incident, from the Garden party was quickly forgotten. Her little transgression had passed by, without impairing her development, or the way I felt about her.

She was evolving before my very eyes, into a gracious young lady. In just few weeks after her coming out, she was presentable enough to accompany me almost anywhere. I took Ciara with me, when running errands, shopping for antiques or just walking. I even took her with me to a couple of dinner engagements, where with the charming exemption of a few stray hairs, she looked and acted perfectly. She was my rose without a thorn and it was I who could take the credit for bringing out all the spiritual and physical perfection in her.

It was at one of those dinners, that I've noticed a couple of young men looking at her across the table. There was sort of a hungry longing in their eyes and they could not disguise it as polite interest. They would stare at Ciara for minutes at the time and seemed unable to look away. She didn't have to carry on a clever conversation, for her warm beauty was enough to recommend her to any one man. Her complexion was the color and smoothness of a ripe peach and her hair had the shiny richness of black silk. Her bosom and waist touched her hips in the most perfect curves, and that without a corset.

It was a little disconcerting to see the effect she had on men, as soon as she walked into a room. For a moment or two, the conversations stalled and the stares reached a level of decided blatancy. If I wasn't sure of her complete innocence in sentimental matters, I might have found some of those men advances worrisome. I was aware that not all of them had honorable intentions, even in my social circles. Fortunately Ciara seemed to pay little heed to their flirting and did not appear to have formed an emotional attachment to any of them. If she was a child, I would have wished for her to never grow up. But she had come to me with the body of a woman and there was nothing I could do to change that.

Colonel Welch, one of the men Ciara met at dinner, seemed especially fascinated by her. He was a man whose morals, people had plenty of reasons to question, but who, not unlike me, had found a new prestige in Egypt. I had heard that his family had disowned him for ruining the reputation of a certain young woman, back in England. Whether that was true or not, he was forced to leave London and provide for himself overseas. He took a respectable enough post in the British army, where many of the prodigal sons have found their place over the years. I might have worried about the Colonel turning his attention to Ciara, since he was well liked by the ladies, but his charm and skill seemed wasted on her. She accepted his advances in a childishly playful manner, understanding their complimentary tone, but acting as if what he said did not concern her at all. The poor colonel, he simply could not understand why his smart flatteries were so poorly understood. He finally gave up, thinking that Ciara simply did not like him. I was beginning to fear that the reason was quite different, and a lot more serious.

It was during that dinner, that I began to realize that my girl didn't have a clear perception of her own identity as a woman. Worse still, perhaps she did not even have the fundamental knowledge of being a human. In my mind, I went over all the troublesome symptoms in her behavior that I have ignored for so long. For one, she would always refer to her self in third person. I disregarded this, thinking that it was just a stage in her development that she would surely reach some day. Then, I remembered how, whenever she would get dressed or have her hair styled, she would not look at herself in the mirror. Or if she did notice her reflection, she would try to touch or smell the woman in the mirror. Maybe I was worried for nothing. Human consciousness was at best a hazy area in human evolution.

The next morning after breakfast, I took Ciara by the hand and led her to the full length mirror placed in the vestibule. She was looking at me, wondering what it was that I wanted from her. I pointed to her reflection and kept saying her name. Instead of recognizing own self, she was again trying to touch the young woman in front of her. Or she kept on peeking behind the mirror to see where she was hiding. She never once, made the fundamental connection between her reflection and herself. This did not diminish one iota my affection for her. She didn't have consciousness of her own being, but I still held hope that she might, one day. Her progress was so amazing in every other area and I was proud of her. I loved her and nothing could change that.

My life had become so predictable that it was a big change in routine when Ciara didn't join me for breakfast on Monday morning. After waiting for more than twenty minutes, I finally sent Kasi upstairs to see what had happened to her. I had to go to work pretty soon and was going to be a pity, not to see my girl before that. It had become a habit for the both of us to have breakfast together and talk. My maid returned in just a couple of minutes, saying that the young mistress wasn't hungry.

"Master Richard," Kasi added. "She looks odd and no sitting still."

"Is she ill?' I asked.

"She says no," Kasi replied. "She says to leave alone and go away."

Than my maid said how surprised she was for Ciara being so rude to her. It really hurt her feelings, since she was someone the young girl always seemed to get along with. At that point in the conversation, I decided to personally find out what was going on. I rushed to her bedroom and began to knock on the door. She did not answer. I knew she was in there, I could hear her moving around!

"Are you okay, sweetheart?" I asked, loudly, hoping to penetrate the wood.

"I am coming in," I declared.

I found her walking around the room, looking sad and confused.

"Heavens," I uttered. "What is wrong?"

"Ciara doesn't know what is...wrong." She replied, between stiff jaws and this time I didn't bother to correct her mistake in referring to herself in a third person.

She looked tired, yet alert, not really sick, but different. She couldn't stay still and I hugged her, whispering words of comfort and reassuring her of my affection. We walked to the armchair, sat and I was holding her in my lap. I began rocking her

[79]

back and forth. She buried her face in my shirt and for some time she seemed calmer. Then slowly, lightly she started rubbing up against me, drawing closer, and licking my face and neck. I felt her warmth; her arms were holding me so tight now that I could not move under her weight. The musk sent of her skin was bittersweet and I felt suddenly weak and disoriented. Her eyes were closed, she was breathing heavily and the feel of her was all I could register. I touched her cheeks, than caressed her neck and slender shoulders. She was moaning now, her arms tightly bound behind my back. Startled by my body's involuntary response, I pushed Ciara away, stepping aside, putting some distance between us. For a moment I could not catch my breath. Her beautiful face angered me, with its look of unexpected, knowing sensuality. I stepped closer than grabbed her by the shoulders and began shaking her violently. My impulse was to hurt her, to strangle her, to wipe out the look of lust on her face so I can forget my own disturbing feelings. At the sight of her head bobbing back and forth, I somehow sobered up, and let go of her. She was standing there with arms, dangling limp on the sides of her body. There was absolute emptiness in her eyes, as she walked away, without saying a word to me. Sweaty and confused, I walked out, closing the door behind me.

I didn't bother having breakfast that morning and just the idea of lunch made my stomach turn over. Nor, was I able to get any decent work done that day, for my mind was constantly going over what had transpired between Ciara and me that morning. By the early afternoon, I knew why she was acting that aggressively strange. I had not come to terms with it, but I knew the reason. She was in heat! That was the only possible explanation for her sudden change of behavior. I guessed it was only normal that her instincts were driving her in this, as they were in everything else. I was not really surprised of what had happened I just found it hard to accept it. I also had to decide what the appropriate course of action was to be under the new circumstances.

What I wanted to do, what I almost did, was truly disturbing to me. I was willing for a moment, to jeopardize my life and endanger my principals, just to have her. She wanted to have me too, but my body was the one thing I could not give her. The mere consideration of it was already taking advantage of the unfortunate, vulnerable state she was in. I hoped to still be able to control my most basic urges. I realized that if I wanted to live with myself, I had to set things straight with her. There was the need to carefully explain to her, that we could never be together, in that carnal way. I must have her understand that I could not ignore my moral beliefs; yet I wanted to preserve our father-daughter relationship intact. It had meant so much to me for so long I could not afford to lose it.

As I was riding my bicycle home, I was feverishly rehearsing my speech, but once I got there, my determination abandoned me. I remembered vividly, the weight of her body on top of mine, how tightly her arms were wrapped around my neck. I could still smell her hair and feel her smooth face. All the prudent words vanished from my head, as I found myself afraid of what might transpire if I was to find her alone. I needed the help of someone sober and completely reliable. Kasi was the perfect candidate for the job.

I asked her to come with me, without explaining in much detail what had happened. I just mentioned the urgent need to talk to Ciara about our relationship. If my maid was with me, things wouldn't feel quite as awkward. I did not have to worry for my disturbing feelings, taking control over my body once again. Kasi and I headed to Ciara's room and I was already beginning to regain some of my composure. I was hoping that the conversation could be kept short and at a certain level of civility.

Kasi and I took turns knocking and placing an ear on the bedroom door. There was no answer. Finally we entered, without being invited. The place was dark, quiet, and seemed abandoned. I took the time to look under and behind every piece of furniture, only to confirm what I was already suspected. Ciara was gone and I had no idea where to. The city of Alexandria was vast and any part of it could be reached easily reached by simply hiring a coach. She had a few pounds in her purse and her stocking drawer. The purse was gone. The European quarter, where we resided, could be explored by foot too. There, as well as anywhere else in the city, there were plenty of rogues, potentially dangerous for a young girl, walking alone and after dark. There was no reliable system in Egypt for locating missing persons and Alexandria was no exception. I had only myself to count on to look for her. Only, I had not the slightest idea where Ciara had gone to, or whether I would ever be able to find her.

CHAPTER NINE

The hot afternoon was turning into a balmy evening and I still had no idea as to where to begin my search. The long hours of pacing in the vestibule, waiting to hear the doorbell ring, hoping to see Ciara walk through the front door, were driving me crazy. I was becoming rather frantic imagining the many misfortunes that could have befallen her. She could have been robbed or violated and I was not there to protect her. I suddenly realized with startling clarity that even though I cared for Ciara so much, I did not really know her. There was not a particular place or a person that she had shown preference for. I obviously did not listen to her chatter with the attention that it merited. Or I would have had a better idea as where she had gone to. What was worse, I rarely talked to her, without constantly correcting her speech and manners. I couldn't imagine my life without her, but I had never once told her what she meant to me. I have always treated her as a child, a beautiful, lovable one, but a child nonetheless. She was my responsibility and I had not prepared her well enough, in how to best cope with people and places in my world. I had planned to do it, but kept procrastinating, thinking that we had plenty of time. I could not have been more wrong. I didn't take good enough care of her and now she was gone.

By the time the twilight painted the windows in dark blue tint, I had already decided that I couldn't wait any longer. Not without doing something. She had taken some money with her, to probably hire a coach. Even if my supposition was correct, that still left the most important question unanswered. Where had she gone? Ciara was familiar with some of the homes and places around our house, but they were too close to warrant the need of transportation. In Egypt, it was considered inappropriate for a lady to go anywhere alone and women weren't admitted in any of the clubs or pubs around here. Therefore, she was either in a private home or wandering the streets somewhere. It was probably the first. Her taking her purse, made it clear to me that she must have had a destination in mind. I was afraid that wherever she was, she would surely stand out and be an easy target for a thief or someone worse than that. I was certainly hoping that she was not roaming the streets of Alexandria, unattended, and at night.

I quickly summoned a few of my neighbors and we joined our servants together, to create a large enough search party to look for Ciara. I didn't need to explain too much to the men, for they all have heard of or met my "poor niece". They considered it quite a common occurrence for a mentally disabled person to wander off.

We quickly came up with a plan of action. We decided it to be reasonable, to start looking at the places she was acquainted with and then widen the circle, hoping to see her or find someone that had seen her. By nine o'clock that night I was pretty sure, that she wasn't at any of the places we had gone together. We had gone and checked every spot I could think of without any luck. She probably was not in any of the private homes in the European quarter either, for someone would have likely seen her going in. My friends and I must have interrogated at least a hundred people in the area. No one remembered seeing Ciara or recognized her by our description. I was becoming more discouraged with every passing hour. The search party, I commissioned, truly covered every street in immediate vicinity to our house; she was nowhere to be seen. If Ciara had gone inside one of the houses sheltering people of British, Greek, or Italian nationalities, then she was probably safe. Any of these families, judging by her clothing would realize that she enjoyed some status in life and would not dare to harm her. They would look for a way to contact me and sooner or later they would be able to do so. Yet, since she had probably taken a coach, she could have gone to some of the really poor regions then she was in big trouble. In that case we were wasting our time looking in the wrong place. Only I had no idea where else to go.

By eleven o'clock, I had to release the men, since the impenetrable darkness was rendering the search pointless. The lack of proper illumination at night in urban areas was another task the British consul was struggling to correct. I returned home, exhausted and worrisome.

"Our girl is gone Kasi!" I cried at the first sight of the old woman. To my surprise she had not yet gone to bed.

"I just know she is in trouble and there is nothing I can do about it." I added.

She did not answer. For a minute it looked as if she wanted to tell me something really important, but then changed her mind.

She mumbled something, about having prepared late dinner for me. She was getting ready to walk out. I grabbed a hold of her shoulders and shook her.

"You know something, don't you?" I yelled impatiently. "You must tell me Kasi, if you know where she is."

Look at me! You must tell me!" I said letting go, aware that I was scaring her to death.

"In last month she has been going walks with Colonel Welch." She replied hesitantly. "No angry Master Richard?" She asked pleadingly. "He is such a handsome man."

"Handsome?" I cried. "Are you mad?"

"Ciara went to see his villa on the Bay." She replied stubbornly. 'He says you could see water from the window."

"Oh, Kasi," I said wearily. "Don't you know he cannot be trusted?"

"I know now." She said it with obvious regret.

"With him she is like a lamb among wolfs," I added, unable to decide what to do next.

"I sorry Master Richard," Kasi cried. "Colonel Welch asked me not to say anything."

Tears were rolling down her cheeks, but I did not feel sorry for her. I felt vindicated to see her suffer as I was.

"I made mistake." She cried again.

"Yes, you did," I was unforgiving. "By now it might be too late to prevent a disaster."

She was sobbing now. I wanted to slap her across the face, so hard that her head would spin.

"Master Richard, forgive foolish, old woman," she said. "I have served you these two years!"

"For God's sake woman, don't you realize what you have done?" I yelled. "I wouldn't leave my dog alone with Colonel Welch."

"You are no better than a Madam in a brothel," I declared, wanting to hurt her. I could care less about her tears and ignored them by walking out.

I didn't have the time, or desire, to summon back my men, which was probably for the best. I had no idea as to what I was going to find at the Colonel's villa. It was far better if I went there alone and dealt with the situation as it was. I shuffled through my personal papers, remembering that Welch had given me his address awhile back. For the first time in my life, I wished I owned a pistol. Would not it be nice to be able to shoot him and thus get even for all the heartache he had already cost me? In the absence of a gun I had to make do with the antique dagger from my collection. It was big enough to demand some respect and sharp enough in case I needed to use in retribution.

I was afraid I was going to be too late. Welch was famous for his excessive drinking, womanizing, and it was rumored that, even here, he had ruined the reputations of several women. I knew from his own boasting that he liked to smoke hashish as well. And that was what people knew. God knows what atrocities was such a man capable of. Ciara was in the wrong place, at the wrong time, with the very wrong man; and the twenty or so miles to my destination, seemed as lengthy as two hundred. In the interest of confidentiality I had decided to not hire a coach, but my bike seemed quite inadequate. I simply couldn't get to my destination fast enough.

The house was in an area, completely outside of the European quarter. In the darkness, I could not tell with complete certainty, but it seemed to be located quite favorable. I could hear the sound of waves and feel the gentle breeze, coming from the ocean. I could wager that during the day the view was amazingly beautiful.

The villa was generously illuminated, filled with laughter and other merry sounds of a celebration going on. I didn't bother straightening my bicycle to the wall, just left it lying on the ground. I did not bother knocking either. I stormed through the front door with steely determination and barged into the dim hallway. I firmly dismissed the young servant's explanation that his master wasn't accepting visitors. I pushed him away and forced my way towards the noise and chatter. The grand dining room was full of drunken officers and some of the filthiest, most unappealing, prostitutes I have ever seen. The unmistakable stench of smoked hashish was so thick, that my eyes had begun watering as I was examining the faces before me. I was shoving my way, through one group or another, ignoring the swearing, angry looks or ugly remarks on my appearance and agitation.

I didn't see Ciara. Colonel Welch wasn't there either and any inquires about their whereabouts were met with ridicule or foolish, drunken aggression. I was finally able to convince one of the women in the room that looked somewhat sober to show me the way to the master bedroom. I didn't knock on that door either.

They were sitting on the large bed very close to one another. Ciara didn't appear to be frightened. She should have been! The man next to her, despite his youth and innocent good looks, wasn't harmless, nor did he have honorable intentions. The bodice of her dress was already unlaced. The soft layers of her skirts were hiked up over the knees and Welch's hand was moving higher on her thigh mauling it with his stubby fingers. Ciara's hair was loose and fell in disarray over her shoulders. The Colonel's other hairy arm was wrapped around her waist, and I clenched my fists, seeing his red moth pressed against her blushed cheek. His hands were so ugly with short fingers and large, hairy knuckles. His face was red flushed with drunken stupor and lust. Seeing him kiss her now bare shoulder with his wet, nasty mouth made me loose the bit of self-control I still possessed.

"She is coming with me!" I said gruffly, walking over to them. They both ignored me.

"Right now!" I insisted, taking Ciara's hand, trying to pull her away from him. He took a minute to focus his drunken gaze on me, and then stood up taller, and heavier, and then I remembered. A couple of glasses and an empty bottle of wine fell on the flour before him.

"She isn't going anywhere!" He mumbled. "Do you hear?" Welch was slurring his words and having difficulty with keeping his balance. That didn't however help me in avoiding his heavy fist. I felt the stone of his large ring tear through my lips and chin. I folded on my knees, warm blood spurting from my nose and mouth. The proud and satisfied look on his face vanished as I struggled to stand up. My punch was so weak and misdirected, that I barely touched his face, before finding myself on the floor again. My head felt as if it was partly separated from the shoulders. I stood up again, slowly, my entire body screaming in agonizing pain.

"I must stay here and fight," was the only coherent thought I could hold on to. "Or he would ravage her."

I had to stay and fight even if he killed me. I couldn't let him have his way with her. I simply couldn't! I knew all too well what had he wanted from her and could not allow it to happen.

The surprised look on his red face turned into blind rage and this time his swing wasn't as well directed as before. Welch was still having trouble keeping his balance and in that I saw my only chance. I invested all my fury, all my pain in one last punch and he fell motionless to the ground. I didn't bother on checking, whether he was still breathing, for I was fairly sure, my swing was not strong enough to kill him. I did not however, resist the shameful temptation of kicking him a couple of times, while he was down. Out of breath, I was swaggering over him and trying to produce enough saliva, so I can spit it on him. It would be a childish, yet extremely satisfying action on my part. It took a minute or two for me to gather enough moisture in my mouth. I was standing there, over the limp body of my rival, half laughing, half trying to concentrate on the task at hand. With the goal of my spiting on him finally achieved. I was ready to go. Ciara was already standing next to me all affection and eager obedience. I had to lean on her to be able to walk out still standing. The amazing feeling of triumph completely overwhelmed the pain from the scratches and bruises on my face.

I do not remember very well my return home. Ciara hailed a coach and I heard her in a fog haggling with the coachmen over the price of the fare. She helped me, almost carried me to my seat. Her presence at my side, heading home was the only clear memory, remaining of that long night.

CHAPTER TEN

Ciara walked me, almost carried me to my bed. She left me for couple of minutes so she can bring me some brandy. I drank it, deeply grateful for the warming, tingling sensation that came rushing through my body. Before falling asleep I could hear Kasi saying that the doctor would arrive in the morning. I must have slept longer than I had anticipated, because it was already late morning when I awoke. Ciara was sitting on a chair next to my bed and I wondered if she had slept a wink. I was so happy to have her with me again and safe. She smiled and began feeding me spoonfuls of goat milk and honey. The taste was absolutely atrocious. I did not have the heart to tell her that I would have much more preferred a cup of hot, black tea.

"Doctor is here," She said when done. "You ready to see him?"

"Send him in," I replied. I was hopeful that Kasi had summoned an Egyptian medic named Makhi. Not only did he have a wide area of expertise, but also he had treated me before and I found him quite capable and very discreet. I would never have considered using a local doctor, when first arriving in the country. However, I soon realized the great advantage of using one which had no contact with any people that knew me. The less information they had of my life and ailments, the better.

Doctor Makhi walked in and his clean appearance and quiet manner were of instant comfort to me. He examined my scratches carefully, checked my pulse and finished by observing the degree of redness on the inside of my eyelids. He gave me a shot of morphine for the pain and assured me, that in a few days I would be as good as new. He promised to visit again in the evening and left without asking any questions as to the cause of my injuries. Nor did he display any misplaced curiosity as to the presence of young Ciara in my bedroom. She had returned when the examination was half over with. She brought some broth and bread and spoon fed those to me, despite my protests of being able to do it myself. The morphine had made me sleepy and I laid back, pleasantly content of being cared for, as if I was a child.

My girl was with me, safe and nothing could ruin the peace I felt. She was still holding my hand, while I was slowly drifting into sleep.

She was by my bed every time I awoke, for three days straight, during the difficult course of my recovery. She was so devoted to me, so eager to please that no task in my care was too hard or made her squeamish. At lunch and dinner she patiently fed me every last morsel of food in bed. Afterwards, she would carefully help me reach the washroom. She gave me a bath, dressed me, and shaved me, all with amazing competence. She would even read the morning paper to me, something still difficult for her, and her effort was absolutely delightful. There was nothing that she wouldn't do for me, even most difficult and unpleasant things, when nursing me back to health. On the first day of my recovery, when I was still feeling very weak, she had to wipe off my bottom. She did not even blink and did it with the same flair with which she would be picking flowers.

She insisted on spoon-feeding me at each meal, which I enjoyed and allowed, since I enjoyed being pampered. For three days, she was doing absolutely everything for me. I realized that surprisingly there was nothing I wished to disguise from her, nothing I did not want to share with her. For the first time in my life, I experienced the amazing freedom of being myself completely and wholeheartedly. Nothing could sever the powerful bond holding us together from that time on.

I began feeling better in a few days and with the passing of each and every hour I was more aware and more intoxicated by Ciara's presence. I've struggled to forget what I had seen that night at Colonel's Welch, but I was continuously haunted by the vision of her smooth, bare shoulders and the soft, dark hair draped over them. I remembered again and again how amazing it to have her body pressing against mine, her breath in my ear, her eyes closed and her face slowly blushing. I could literally follow the blood rushing to her earlobes and coloring them the soft pink color of a seashell. Suddenly, I felt very tired of always running away from what I really wanted. I felt exhausted of always having to consider the consequences of my actions. I was discontent with my life such as it was and kept thinking of how wonderful it must be to not be accountable. I wanted just once to do something spontaneous, to experience something wild, even dangerous.

Maybe Ciara and I were meant to come together in a truly physical way. We certainly were very much together spiritually. It might be glorious. With all the others the act was never that. As soon as I had gotten what I wanted I was out of there. I felt guilty and sometimes reminded of what I was forced to endure from the hands of another man. What my stepfather had done to me were things I was desperately trying to forget. With someone I loved it would be different. I could feel it in my heart. I longed to surrender to love and finally satisfy that hungry emptiness inside.

That evening, five days after Ciara ran away, when she walked into the room with my dinner, I gently pushed the tray away. I drew her in bed next me, inhaling the familiar musky smell of her. My overwhelming desire for her felt so right. I hadn't the power, nor did I wish to fight against it any longer. I took her tiny, delicate hand and brushed with my lips the pulsating softness of the inside of her wrist. I wrapped my hands around her waist and my fingers almost touched. I was gently kissing her face, her eyes, and her sensual mouth. She pressed herself against me and could fell the warm globes of her bosoms. I was caressing her smooth, long neck, and strong arms. She was on top of me the

dark cloud of her hair enveloping my face, invading all my senses.
I pinned her down, feeling the need to dominate her. She allowed
me to do this and her body responded with passion to every caress,
stroke and kiss. I began removing her clothing, piece by piece
slowly revealing her lean, flexible body. I was mesmerized by
every part of her slowly emerging, each one suddenly new,
unfamiliar and exciting. Her eyes stayed open the whole time,
glowing in the darkness with the yellow, startling gleam of a wild
predator. Her skin felt hot and sleek under my eager fingers and I
was breathing in the sent of her hair, feeling as if it was the very air
I needed to survive. The many long months of suppressed desire,
merging with her passionate response to my touch, turned those
sleepless hours into one unforgettable night. Reality and dream
swirled together in the shape of this unbelievable creature, making
me ache for her in a way I had never known before. I longed for
her and possessed her over and over again. I felt complete only
and when Ciara and I were merged into one.

It must have been close to morning when I finally fell
asleep. I wished I had slept without dreaming. The horrible
nightmare forced me to jump out of my bed, feeling hot and

disoriented. I couldn't remember the dream in its entirety, but I remembered clearly how I felt. I was standing on a rocky, tiny piece of land amongst dark, raging waves of the sea. I was a very young boy alone, lost and terrified. I was crying and calling out for my mother but somehow I knew she would not answer. Then I saw a boat, that slowly emerged from the fogy mist and I shrieked that I was there, waving my hands, to the people on board to see me and save me. Elisabeth was in the boat, she looked at me and laughed, turning her back to me, and then suddenly it wasn't Elisabeth, but my mother. As always, she looked at me without really seeing me and I knew what she thought without her even having to say it. She thought that I was not worth saving.

For many years, I have struggled to forget my now long dead mother and what my life with her was like. So, I wondered where this disturbing nightmare was coming from. Was it sign for things to come? A warning from above, that I would be cursed forever for what I had done with Ciara? Was I a monster, for taking advantage of her? I only knew that I suddenly felt guilty and confused. I was no longer sure that what I had done felt right or was morally justified. Blinding pain kept on pounding on both sides of my head and everything seemed so altered now, under the sobering light of the morning. I realized with some relief that Ciara was gone from my bed and I did not rush to go after her. I did not know if I could bear looking her straight in the eyes just now. All these years, I had considered my stepfather to be a monster, for what he had done to me. And now it seemed to me that I had done exactly what I despised him so much for. I had taken advantage of her. Whether she wanted me too or not was beside the point. She was my charge and I was supposed to take care of her and treat her as a beloved daughter, nothing else. The fact that we were not truly related was also insignificant. She was a small child in a woman's body or even an innocent animal in a human shape. At any case, she was not truly capable of consenting to what transpired between us last night.

I was drowning in the bitter waters of regrets, guilt, and fear and there was little hope of coming out still intact. The lump in my throat was making it hard to breathe. It had become clear to me that I had a lot of conflicting feelings about Ciara. I had to somehow, find a way to keep them balanced and under control. I've indulged with her a dark and primitive side of my nature. I vowed to myself to never do it again. For God's sake, I had presented her to everyone as my niece! What if people were to find out? I had in the spur of the moment put my future, my entire life, on the line! For one night of pleasure, I was ready to sacrifice everything. I was beginning to think it was not worth it. After all, I've worked too hard to build this life, to let anyone, including myself destroy it. I didn't know if Ciara understood the full magnitude of what had happened. Regardless, I had to make sure she accepted that there was not going to be a repeat of last night. No matter the circumstances. All I could hope for the time being was that no one would find out about our carnal encounter. I wanted to forget about it as soon as possible and was only praying for her to be able to do so, as well.

Since Ciara was not in the bed next to me when I awoke, I assumed that she went back to her room, where she would be more comfortable. It was urgent to talk to her as soon as possible and have things settled once and for all in a familiar routine. I was considering the best way to inform her of my decision, while washing my face and hands. The stubble on my chin was unattractive and irritating. I nicked myself shaving and wiped the tiny droplet of blood, looking closer in the washroom mirror. The visage staring back at me was that of an old and tired man. I never particularly liked my face, pale and freckled as it was, with a longish nose and receding hairline. It looked even worse to me on that day, with dark, puffy circles under the eyes and lips raw and red from kisses. I haven't even reached forty yet, what was there to be tired of? But I was already feeling aged before my time, as if there was not much I had to look forward to. I felt I have seen it all.

I sighed and began getting dressed; brushing my hair, and coarse mustache, pretending that nothing had changed. All I could do for myself was to look somewhat decent. I wanted to talk to Ciara before breakfast, since that was one of the few times during the day when we could be completely alone. Despite my emotional state, I was ravenous and was secretly hoping that our conversation wouldn't take too long.

I walked into her bedroom, barely acknowledging the fact that I didn't bother to knock. Was I forgetting my manners because it was my house, or was I that casual because I had possessed her? Ciara was sleeping peacefully in her own bed and her resting face was truly angelic with its soft, relaxed features. She looked innocent, young, and somehow completely untouched. She must have sensed my presence in the room, because she opened her eyes lazily, stretching her body in the usual graceful and sleek manner I so admired. She yawned and I could see the speed bumps on the roof of her mouth and the small, pink curl of her tongue. Light tremors ran through Ciara's limbs, her entire body participating in the gradual ritual of her awakening. She drew herself up slowly, letting out a sigh, the very picture of perfect health and physical satisfaction. She acted very casual, walking towards me. She licked my nose, but in the old playful way and I held her chin up, searching on her face for any memory or understanding of last night. I did not find it. There was no trace or mention of our one lustful encounter. She was behaving as if nothing had happened. There were no questions, regrets, or tears. I did not detect even the slightest change in her attitude. Ciara's period of heat had obviously ended and with it her wanting me. She was once again the carefree, happy child I had always known. There wasn't a single thing I needed to explain or clarify to anyone and the least to her.

I left her in private to get dressed and patiently waited for her in the vestibule, so I can accompany her to the dining room. We had breakfast together and she showed an admirable appetite. I too, obeyed the urge to try every single item on the table. The spread was as always rich and plenty. I had ham and eggs, then sausage, then more tea, finishing with some grapes and cheese. My feeling of relief was so completely overwhelming; that I convinced myself that I wasn't disappointed.

CHAPTER ELEVEN

Later on, I would always divide my life in two parts. The first, before I came together with Ciara and the second after that when everything changed. Everything changed for me in any case. My girl seemed to have moved on, but I was unable to. The knowledge of what had happened was such a burden to me, that I even considered confessing everything to Elisabeth. I was well aware that the impulse driving me was the fervent desire to relief my conscience. Still every day I had to fight the strange and dangerous urge to confess everything to my fiancé. I knew well if I did she would never forgive me for the rest of my days. There were too many lies that I have told, concerning Ciara. At the same time, not only was I feeling guilty I was terrified of people finding out. I could vividly imagine the scandal if it became clear that I had come to know my "niece", in the biblical sense. I kept reminding myself that there was no way of anyone knowing of the incident. It was not as if my girl and I were going to shout it out to the world. All I had to do was stay put and let it go myself. That was easier said than done. I was Ciara's mentor; she was still in my charge, and most days I could behave as if I had forgotten that one night. During the day I kept myself busy with work and occasional social engagements. The time would pass by, having some resemblance of an ordinary routine. Nights were an entirely different matter. They were almost always full with the images of her body, with the softness of her skin and the sent of her hair. My longing for her, my loneliness were so overwhelming, that night after night I had to fight the urge to go to her. Many times I stood before her door, miserable for not going in, yet still incapable to step over the threshold. My bed turned into the most sophisticated torture chamber, and tossing and turning were my frequent visitors in those dark hours. I realized, with mixed emotions, that Ciara didn't seem to recall, or wanted to remember, what had happened between us that one time. And some part of me was secretly hoping that one day she would remember. Why should I be the only one suffering? It was not fair that she was so carefree in her amnesia and I tried so hard to forget but could not.

The frequent lack of adequate sleep and all the disconcerting emotions were naturally beginning to affect my work, as well as my personal life. My superiors had already expressed their dissatisfaction with my job performance. It took a lot to get reprimanded in my field and I was afraid that I was a straw away from severally damaging my carrier. It seemed that all the sacrifices and struggles I've endured in the quest for achieving a good status in life, were coming to nothing. I have also once more, neglected Elisabeth and she was very clear in expressing her displeasure. She was pressing me to choose a wedding date sooner than we had planned and seemed very annoyed at my indecisiveness.

"I do not want to seem too forward," she said at one of our, by that time, rare lunches. "But you seem to show an apparent lack of interest in our life together."

I did not know what to answer. I was not exactly surprised that she had noticed. She was too perceptive and I was too unhappy to be able to adequately conceal from her my emotional turmoil.

She further expressed her dissatisfaction of my not sharing or confiding to her. Trouble was I have never felt her more foreign then at that time. The feeling of camaraderie and common aims we had once shared was now gone. Besides, there was no way of honestly telling her what was bothering me.

Elisabeth gave me plenty of time for an answer, but I was still struggling in finding the right words.

"Richard," she said firmly, putting her fork down. "We must get married within the year."

Then she added with apparent irony, "Or I shall begin to question the extent of your devotion to me."

"We shall get married sooner then," I said with little enthusiasm. I could see she was not convinced in my sincerity. I took her hand and kissed it, half heartedly at best.

"I am sorry, my dear." I said wearily. "I feel a little tired."

"Get some sleep." She said patting my hand, as I was escorting her to the door. Her next question startled me.

"I must know if you have any doubts or…if there is someone else?" Her voice betrayed her feelings this time. It was trembling.

She looked me straight in the eye, holding the handle of her beige parasol, her knuckles almost white from the force of her grip.

I felt warm blood rushing to my face and the cold, uncomfortable wetness, lingering on the palms of my hands.

"There is no one else Elisabeth," I said, with a sudden surge of energy. I was not looking at her. I almost believed myself I was telling her the truth.

She nodded, seeming satisfied with my flimsy assurance. I felt the lowest, most dishonorable man on Earth for having to lie to her, but I had no choice. I certainly didn't want to hurt her. She didn't deserve to suffer for my transgressions.

"Do you have any doubts, in regards of marrying me?" She insisted.

She was a fool asking all those questions. I might feel compelled to really answer them this time.

"I haven't asked, if you loved me Richard," she added calmly.

"Love is not a useful emotion for people like you and me," she continued, oblivious to my frustration. "I must know if you still want to…still want to…" She paused, trying to compose herself. I could have sworn I saw tears in her eyes. But Elisabeth never cried!

"Most certainly I do! You have nothing to be concerned about!" I said hurriedly.

"My health has not been the best of late." I added, hoping to change the subject. "Are you having second thoughts?" I asked her. I have learned long ago that, often, offence was the best defense. It worked.

She abandoned all of her concerns in her eager attempt to convince me of her devotion. I finally walked her out and she left the Club, I was hoping reassured of my loyalty. I was mad at myself. Her not so unexpected questions had found me somehow unprepared. It was time to pull myself together and shape up. If I kept up with the way I was acting, it would be only a matter of time before my odd behavior becomes apparent to everyone. I did not feel capable of dealing with the potential scandal. It was time to get myself out of that mess I have created and it was time for me to reconsider my attitude.

The first step for this to work was to become content with my life, the way it was, and was going to be. Tolerable career, Elisabeth as my wife, respectable home in England some day, and a good social life. Ciara and I, we couldn't possibly have any future together. I guess I have always known that. It was pointless to treasure lingering memories of her touch and how it made me feel any more. I couldn't change the way things were. She had her place in life and I had mine, and they weren't equal. Our paths were never to cross again as man and a woman. I felt so tired of all those feelings of guilt and regret. I was exhausted from tossing and turning in bed every single night. It was time to cease with my desperate longing for her; it was beginning to drive me completely insane. What had been between us was over with and I struggled to convince myself that it was better that way.

The second step, for that to work, was to rise to the challenge and take extreme measures to rectify the situation. I had to give up the luxury of seeing Ciara in private if I wanted her and myself safe from an eventual repeat of that one night.

From that moment on Kasi came with me, each time I went to see my girl. The two women at least, were plenty happy with my visits being organized in that way. As time went by, the both of them seem to develop an even deeper affection for each other. The two women were becoming closer with each passing day. Kasi was already very protective of the young girl and soon I began thinking that she suspected that something happened between Ciara and me. In any case, she was watching me even closer and I was certain that if I had not asked her to keep me company on my visits, she would have soon volunteered to do so herself. I was already feeling uneasy of demonstrating too much attention to the young girl, so I took that chance in withdrawing from her life almost completely.

The two women did not seem to miss me much. Soon they began spending all of their free time together. I often saw the both of them reading books, singing songs or playing together in the garden. My role in their lives was quickly becoming quite insignificant. One morning I found Kasi taking paper and quills out of my study, without asking for permission. When I asked her, in a bad temper, what she needed them for, she looked at me as if I was an idiot.

"Ciara wants them." She said. "I think she is writing diary."

"What are you talking about?" I said irritably. "She can't even write that well, how could she keep a diary?" I was feeling very agitated.

"I don't know, Master." She answered, urging to go. "I know she asked for the paper. Do you want me to take it back to study?" She asked timidly, but her eyes were sparkling with suppressed laughter.

"It does not matter! Take it to her, if she wants it." I said angrily. "It would be perhaps a waste, but go ahead, carry on."

Not too long ago my girl would've asked me for those items. I was the one who taught her how to read and write. Was it possible that she was in fact keeping a diary? I doubted it. She could not write that well yet. Or may be she could and I just did not know? One thing was for certain, she was replacing me with ease, and I couldn't help but feel disappointed about it. I wanted to keep some emotional distance between us, I just never realized she was going to cope with it that well. I was missing our old closeness and understanding. I guess I did not want her to share everything with me I just wanted her to still need me sometimes. I missed the way she used to run to me, as if I was the only person in the whole world. It used to be that she was ecstatic to see me. Now, it seemed to me that she couldn't care less if she saw me at all.

I wished I could say that her coldness made matters easier to me. Instead, I was beginning to rehash things, more and more, every day. My plan to get myself out of my complicated domestic situation was not working out very well. So, I buried myself in my work. I spent more and more time there. There was no one waiting for me to come home. My superiors quickly acknowledged my renewed efforts to excel in my job. Elisabeth was pleased as well with my fresh attempts to be with her. I was spending more and more time with my fiancée, enjoying the renewed, yet fragile closeness between us. I was scarcely spending any time with Ciara, at that point, and made sure I was never again to be alone with her. Still, all my honorable efforts would've been fruitless if I had not had an epiphany and decided to get away.

"It is the only thing left to do," I assured myself. Putting some miles between Ciara and me would help me to completely rid myself of the spell she had over me. After all, for the two years I had spent in Egypt I had not once taken a vacation. I could certainly use a break as well as change of scenery. The hot and dusty Egyptian summer had arrived and even Alexandria was becoming unbearable. British government officials were always encouraged to spend their two-month leave in England, in part because of the cooler climate, and also because many of them had families there. I did not any longer. However, this time it was absolutely mandatory to go, as the only way to achieve some kind of a closure in my domestic troubles. I might not have the proper connections in London, but Elisabeth most certainly did.

She was absolutely thrilled that we were going to spend the summer together in England. We had never before spent that much time exclusively in each others company. We planned to sail on a steamship named "The Swallow", which would depart from the Port of Alexandria on the fifteenth of June. When in London, we were going to stay at the house of Elisabeth's uncle, Sir Howard Boyle. The lodging was described to me as one fit for a king. Sir Boyle was very well respected and absolutely dotted on his niece. I was excited at the prospect of being exclusively in the company of ladies and gentlemen, only of the best breeding and state in life. The idea of leaving Egypt for even two months was suddenly extremely appealing. I prepared for the trip hastily, determined to think of nothing, and no one else, I might be leaving behind.

The morning of the fifteenth promised to be extremely hot and humid. I woke up early to once more check my luggage and make sure that I had not forgotten anything. I supervised the loading of the coach, while I was thinking about Ciara. I had politely inquired after her, the night before my departure. She was late showing up for our farewells, and appeared cold and distant, as she had been of late. Her manner convinced me completely, that I wouldn't be greatly missed. I was obviously doing the right thing. I was already seeing the vacation as my only salvation from her. And all those disturbing feelings of mine that threatened to destroy my comfortable and safe existence.

CHAPTER TWELVE

Elisabeth and I began our long journey back to England with a lot of excitement and very good spirits. Her companion, Ms. Lane, was a lady in her fifties and sometimes neglected her duties of a chaperone, complaining of fatigue and achy joints. She was also unfortunate enough to succumb to suffering from seasickness, a condition that my fiancé and I were able to avoid thus far. So, the engaged couple was often left to walk in privacy on board and explore the ship. Entertainment was limited and often consisted of having meals with the Captain, named Gordon Wallis, and selected few others of the crew. The time spent on the ship was priceless for Elisabeth and me. For the first time since we had gotten engaged, we could talk in depth about life and ourselves. It was quiet and there were not many distractions and I liked it that way. I used to worry, if the both of us had anything to say to each other if we were ever to be left to our own means too.

Of course, we were plenty busy, once we arrived in Europe. En route to Great Britain, we meandered through Greece, Italy, and

France, and only stayed at the best inns along the way. Elisabeth's father had made sure of that. We spend a few days in each country, taking in the sights and enjoying the scenery, then taking another steam ship, continued on our way.

Ever since we left Egypt I was breathing easier and not only because of the cooler weather. It was like a heavy weight had been lifted of my shoulders and I was beginning to defeat all the conflicting emotions, tearing me apart not that long ago. I finally felt free to enjoy myself. I was embracing the many colorful sides of all the different cultures, but still enjoyed all the comforts given to an Englishman with some money. Elisabeth seemed to have a good time as well. She appeared freer and more joyful in Europe and I suddenly found her once again an interesting, if not exactly desirable, lady.

We tasted many exotic foods and gourmet wines in fashionable restaurants or enjoyed the particular country's plainer national cuisine in pubs. And not once, did I have to worry about how much I was spending for Mr. Boyle had given us letters of credit that were good anywhere in the world.

Surprisingly, I found myself capable of appreciating the unique sort of entertainment each place had to offer, and found each one fascinating on its own merit. Elisabeth and I spent many hours taking leisurely walks and exploring the astonishing architecture of Greece. We had many long conversations about Renaissance art and literature in Italy. We discovered our tastes to be so splendidly similar, discussing the controversial works of modernists in France. We shared an easy admiration for the thorough perfection of the Castle in Versailles, or the sleek, powerful lines, of the Acropolis in Athens. We found both places somewhat imposing though. Even our political views were the same, for we completely supported the British Colonial Policy and believed in the superiority of the ruling class. As we discussed politics, culture, and what we both wanted out of life, I was beginning to really like Elisabeth. We continued talking straightforwardly, and honestly, in a way we never had before. I was delighted with the newfound emotional closeness between us and proud of her polished manner and sober intelligence. I tried really hard not to compare my fiancée and Ciara, for I felt that it would not be fair to either of them.

After two very pleasant weeks en route we, finally reached the Plymouth's port of entry and from here we were to continue to London via coach. I was sorry to see our sea voyage end. I really had had wonderful time. Elisabeth and I had the great opportunity to stay in one of the best parts of town. Sir Howard Boyle owned a formidable house on the western side of the city, far enough from Cheapside. From the windows one could enjoy the fresh, green branches of Hide Park and the summer air was fresh and fragrant from all that greenery. The garden was huge and full with many exotic plants and flowers. Sir Howard was determined to be the perfect host. He was extremely fond of my fiancée, since he had no children of his own, so thanks to her he treated us delightfully. He mentioned several times during dinner that evening that after his death, she and our children would inherit his sizable estate with the right to run it in any way she saw fit.

Sir Boyle also expressed his ardent intentions to hold a ball for Elisabeth and me as a way to celebrate our engagement anew in London. The grand event was scheduled sometime at the end of our visit and I saw it as and the opportunity to better my connections and happily converse with so many agreeable ladies and gentlemen. Finally, I could communicate with people on my intellectual and social level.

That was most certainly the life I always wanted to live; and one I felt I deserved. The house held every possible comfort known to man and it was filled with servants, eager to please. It was customary to change our clothes for the afternoon tea, then once more for dinner. We often spent our evenings having dinner with other families, always distinguished ones, or attending theater or musical performances in Covent Garden or the Italian Opera House. I got used to waking up late and the young maid bringing me my breakfast and morning paper in bed, along with fresh set of perfectly pressed clothes.

My one and only job for the day was to choose where to go or what to do for entertainment. Our days were lazy and sometimes spent in one of the many fashionable coffeehouses where we took our lunch. Sometimes Elisabeth and I would meet some friends there but often it was just the two of us. Her chaperone, Ms Lane, was almost always absent, yet Sir Boyle seemed to hold firm to the unconventional belief that his niece could take care of herself and did not seem to mind. Of course,

Elisabeth was almost thirty and I was most certainly not the kind of man, which would take advantage of her innocence before the wedding.

I soon familiarized myself once more with all the main streets, running through the city and became quite comfortable in town. The only part, I was determined to avoid at all costs was naturally Cheap Side, where I was born. I did not need to be reminded of where I had come from or where a humbler portion of Londoners lived. Not that there was any danger of Elisabeth requesting to see it. She knew enough of my past not to ask any unnecessary questions, but there were things I could never share with her. It would be too much reality for her to take, despite the fact that our relationship was better than ever.

I sometimes wondered if the house I grew up in was still standing. It deserved to be leveled to the ground. It was an unimaginable place of horrors where my stepfather came to my bedroom almost every night. I still had nightmares of the things he did to me. I had always believed that my mother could, but chose not to see, what was happening. I used to wonder as a young boy whom I hated more, him or her. At the end they both seem to quiet their consciences with my step-father agreeing to pay for my education at Cambridge.

My beloved grandmother was the only one who seemed to suspect that something was wrong, although I was too embarrassed to say anything to her or anyone else. Nonetheless, she made sure I spent as much time in her tiny house as I possibly could. After her passing, I used to lay awake at night and think that if I died, no one would shed a single tear.

I had not known my father for he had died long before I was old enough to truly remember him. He was a cavalry officer and a man, who found domestic bliss with my mother so unappealing that he only endured it for a couple of years. My mother spoke of him with bitterness and contempt, for he made a modest living and failed to offer her the life she felt she deserved. She wanted to be rich and respected, regardless of the fact she was the only daughter of humble merchants. Her modest dowry and short lived infatuation with my father prevented her from reaching that goal. That was a mistake she was determined to correct with her second marriage. My stepfather was not handsome or nice, but wealthy enough to make her very happy. To her delight, there were no children of the marriage and that absence was one of the few things we agreed upon.

My mother died when I had just finished college and I did not attend her funeral. I was of age than and free to do as I pleased. My stepfather was the one person that I hoped to never see again as long as I lived. Many times, I resisted the dangerous urge to find out what had come of him. I knew well that this knowledge would not bring me any closure. The one thing I could do for was building a good life of my own and marrying well. I was determined to do so, for I had endured enough ridicule and spite from classmates with only higher birth than mine. Most of them were not nearly as clever and capable as I was, yet they still despised me. It would be grand to be respected, to finally and truly fit in. So, I was thrilled at the opportunity to work as an engineer in India at the ripe age of 26. The country had been a British protectorate for some time and there I was enjoying a better social status, since Englishmen were considered far superior to Indian. That status was accompanied by a tolerable salary as well. I spent several years there and quickly realized that I was still not treated as an equal among my compatriots. The only way I could achieve that, was to marry up. I did not get this opportunity in India and the only path left open to me was to work hard and swallow my bitterness. I was being promoted at a far slower rate, than some of my colleagues. Still, I considered my experience in the country invaluable, since it afforded me the opportunity to receive my present work assignment in Egypt.

I arrived in the country in 1886 and having little illusions as to how hard I had to work to succeed. Then I met Elisabeth and things got a lot easier. Two years had gone by and I was well on my way to returning to England as a respectable man, with great marriage and with good social status.

During my glorious vacation in London, I congratulated myself every day on making such a suitable match. I felt renewed gratitude for Elisabeth's consent to marry poor old me. My fiancée was best chance I to turn things around in my life and I was determined to never again endanger our relationship. Ciara was only a faint memory now and I could deal with ease now with the prospect of putting her into a home. Not even two months had gone by and I was wondering what was so special about her that used to keep me awake at night. Surely, she was sensually beautiful, but I was no longer the kind of man to dither by that beauty from the path he had taken.

The evening of Elisabeth's and my Engagement Ball arrived and I did not feel even a bit jittery, but was in a rather calm and pleasant state of mind. The wealth and grandness of the event and our surroundings deepened even more my feelings of personal gratification. My hungry ego was satisfied. All this was going to be ours one day!

The ball was being held in the Grand hall of the home, and faithful to its name, it was imposingly spacious. For dinner, Sir Howard had truly outdone himself. Fifteen or so sweet and savory dishes were catered in and displayed in geometric patterns on the long mahogany table. The latter, was decorated with heaps of fresh flowers; the white linen adorned with the finest china, polished silver ware, and meticulously carved crystal glasses and canisters.

Several highly accomplished ladies and distinguished gentlemen were present that evening, and I made an effort to present myself in the best possible light. Elisabeth took her role as a hostess very much to heart, since her uncle was not married and there was no one else to take on that duty. The dinner went by without a glitch. The ceremonial announcement of our engagement was given the utmost attention and we were showered in well wishes, by the time an assortment of deserts had arrived.

The ball followed the dinner right after the table and chairs had been cleared. The guests could now better appreciate the marble floors and crystal chandeliers, so bright, that they were turning the night into a day. Elisabeth and I as the happy couple were most certainly the center of attention and we danced almost every dance with each other. Exceptions were made only when following of the proper customs was required and we had to graciously dance with some of the other guests. A great show was made out of Elisabeth dancing the last waltz with her uncle. Afterwards, Sir Howard informed me as to how pleased he was for the time he had spent with both of us. He insisted on us visiting him regularly after the wedding, something I was thrilled to promise to him.

The evening was concluded at midnight and after seeing the guests on their way we all promptly retired to our sleeping quarters. Elisabeth seemed deep in happy thoughts, I assumed about our wedding. I, on the other hand, was focused on the eve of our return to Egypt to look for a way of suitable addressing my domestic situation. The time had come for our so-called liaison to end one way or another.

She was the only one now, standing between me and the life I intended to live and the only one capable of destroying it. I was afraid I would want her still, especially if we lived together. After all, for her, I was clearly capable of ignoring my better judgment. She was dangerous for me, very much so and the only solution was to put her away. I still disliked the idea of putting her into a home for people with mental disabilities. So my only remaining option was that of finding a nice Egyptian family that would take care of Ciara in exchange for some money. I have heard of other Englishmen doing so under somewhat similar circumstances and I regretted not paying more attention to the particulars in those cases. I should be able to find a decent childless couple, living maybe somewhere in the country, with which my "niece" could be quite happy. If things turned out the way I had planned, I would still be taking care of her, yet there would be safe distance between us.

One way or another I was going back to Egypt a new man, determined to follow through with my plan and ignore any useless emotions that might get in the way.

CHAPTER THIRTEEN

Our return back to Egypt was plagued with troubles from the very beginning and was not nearly as pleasant as the first part of our trip had been. By the time Elisabeth and I had reached Plymouth and were ready to sail, turbulent storms had begun ravaging the Mediterranean. It was near the end of August and I was assured that it was not a storm season yet, and the bad weather should quit in a day or two. Then a whole week had gone by and there was no sign of that happening any time soon. I was due to be back at work on the tenth of September. My vacation had been allowed to last longer than usually permitted, because Elisabeth had written to the Department of Public Works. I was given three weeks extra of time off, but it was absolutely mandatory to be back on the scheduled date, and no excuses would be accepted.

Because of the weather several of the better steamships were taking a wait and see attitude and were not ready to sail as of yet. I got the same answer from all the captains I had gone to discuss my predicament with. They were adamant, that not only it would be uncomfortable for passengers who chose to travel then, but potentially very dangerous. The stormy waters and cloudiness would affect, to an unknown extent, the length of the trip, as well as the quality of the visibility. I was even told by one very weathered seaman, that even one's compass tended to misbehave in those circumstances.

Unfortunately, I was due back to work in less than a week and did not have the luxury of waiting. Thus I had to find out if any ship was sailing and if so, take it no matter the circumstances. To my surprise Elisabeth insisted on traveling with me.

"Do you not want to wait here with Ms. Lane?" I asked. "The both of you can take The Swallow" back to Egypt as soon as the storms clear."

"I would rather go back with you." She said warmly.

So, feeling quite flattered I set out to visiting the Port each morning, hoping to find a ship, ready to brave the stormy waters. Finally I found this tiny vessel, ironically called "The Virgin Queen." It was not the most presentable kind of ship, but the Captain, named Stubbs was ready to sail in a day. He seemed confident enough in his capability to take us back to Egypt in one piece and on time for me to go back to work. I went back to the inn, where we were staying for the time being and informed Ms. Lane and Elisabeth that we were going the next day. The old bitty grumbled endlessly about me putting their lives in danger, but Elisabeth seemed eager to go. She must have been remembering the pleasant days we had spent when on the "The Swallow."

I began to fear that she regretted her decision to come with me the moment the three of us set foot on board of the shaky vessel. When I had hired it to take us back home I had not noticed how unkempt it had been. The ship was so unclean that the dirt had become an essential part of everything around us. It was very small and it took me only couple of minutes to explore it, from one end to the other. The Captain and his crew was a rowdy bunch, often drunk and always rude. Captain Stubbs had the audacity to charge us full fare, yet he and his men were more interested in caring for the contraband they had on board, than for the well being of their passengers. Still Elisabeth and Ms Lane had the good fortune to reside in the only decent cabin on board. Their place was cleaner than the rest of the ship and the two women were able to enjoy some privacy. I, on the other hand, was forced to sleep in a very uncomfortable bunk and have the cook as my roommate. His "quarters" had the unmistakable stench of sour cabbage and cheep gin and I had a strong suspicion that he often neglected to empty his chamber pot. Captain Stubbs and crew were shamelessly drunk for the most of the trip, not that they would've been much help to us if sober. The ship seemed to constantly change direction and I was beginning to fear that they might never find their way. The three of us were the only passengers on board and were left most of the tome to fend for ourselves.

I did not know if the reason was all my worries or whether the dreadful conditions on the ship were the culprit but for the first time in my life I became seasick. The food was intolerable anyway and soon I wasn't able to keep anything down. Even the smell of toast made my stomach turn and there was nothing else, served on board that would not make even a healthy person sick. The only way I was able to have some water or tea was to slurp it slowly with a teaspoon and with caution. I was completely unable to swallow anything but couple of morsels of an apple with the skin peeled off. I was feeling so ill on most days that I did not even attempt to abandon my cabin. I was staying in my dirty, uncomfortable bunk, feeling miserable and too sick to even move. The stormy waters kept tossing the tiny ship around as if it was an empty walnut shell. There was so little in my stomach that I was amazed and exhausted of my body's efforts to still force it out. Sometimes after the dry hives have ceased, I would lay back down, feeling that every tiny muscle in my body was screaming in trembling pain.

The little boy, named Sam that was tending to my needs, looked almost as exhausted as me by the end of the week. Elisabeth on the other hand, was feeling fine and spent her time playing bridge with Ms. Lane and some of the higher up members of the crew. She would have dinner with Captain Stubbs on most nights and seemed to have made the best of the bad situation we were all in. For her, the men had managed to dig out a small table, tea set and even some sugar for her tea. It appeared that a lot of extras have been added to her cabin and the Captain was constantly checking to make sure the women were comfortable. No one but Sam even bothered to see if I needed anything. Elizabeth had stopped by for a visit only once and stayed for not even an hour.

Granted, I was not inclined to keep on with light conversations, nor did I smell like spring flowers then. Still, I believed she should have done a little bit more than just giving couple of shillings to the boy to take care of me. For the rest of the time I was left to suffer alone and was beginning to feel quite bitter for it.

I found it rather odd and very unfair that no one else on board had succumbed to seasickness. Even in bad weather, traveling by steamboat is usually a comfortable enough experience. I had a lot of time to think on that trip, for they were no distractions. I often wondered if my anxiety for what awaited me in Egypt was not the true reason behind my symptoms. I also was not exactly confident in the Captain Stubbs and his crew to take us safely back home.

My mind was finally put to rest when "The Virgin Queen" reached to Port of Alexandria on the seventh of September. I was forced to get up, wash myself and dress to the best of my ability at that moment. My knees were shaking, as Sam escorted me off the ship. I was leaning heavily on his skinny shoulders and he seemed happy to see me go. The moment my feet touched the "terra firma" of the Harbor the terrible nausea vanished. If I had any strength left, I would have kneeled down and kissed the ground.

I sincerely thanked God for bringing me home in one piece. I had lost so much weight in a week that my jacket was hanging loose on me, and I had fastened my belt on the last notch. I felt weak and disoriented and completely incapable of attending to our luggage at the moment. Luckily, Elizabeth soon took matters into her own hands and began issuing orders while taking me by the crook of the arm. The blazing sun almost blinded me, as I stumbled next to her up the pier. Without any help of mine, she managed to hire a sizable coach, one comfortable enough for the hour long ride home. Elisabeth had already decided as to how our luggage to be arranged on the back.

"Go," she said curtly to the coachman and sat back with a satisfied look on her face. Then her eyes met mine. The content smile on her face was replaced by the usual controlled expression of polite indifference. Something else was lurking beneath it though, something I could not quite read. Was it contempt for my apparent inability to take care of things as a man should? Or was she feeling compassion for me in the pathetic, sickly state I was in?

We remained silent inside, thinking our own thoughts, for the ride home. Anyway, I was feeling too tired to worry if she was disappointed in me. I was happy that we did not talk. Once we reached her house I somehow crawled out of the coach and managed to kiss her goodbye. I was back in my place even before Elisabeth's luggage was taken down. She walked into the building, without looking back. Why should she? She seemed completely capable of taking care of herself, so I intended to let her do just that.

I ordered the coachmen to take me home and sat back feeling somewhat restored. I was anxious to get home and rest in my own bed, one sat firmly on a steady ground. Finally I would be under the gentle care of my maid. I was certain that with some proper food and rest I would feel better quickly.

CHAPTER FOURTEEN

I could see the roof of my house from the coach we were less than a mile away from home. The coach reached my street and I could barely contain my excitement. It felt good to travel, but even better to be back. I felt as if I had been away for an eternity. I had not realized how much I had missed my house with all of my things in it.

Kasi was waiting for me outside, on the porch somehow aware of the exact time of my arrival home. She was as eager to please and nurturing as always. If it would not be considered inappropriate I would have kissed her. She helped me to my bedroom right the way, where I could clean up and change into fresh clothes. I walked out almost feeling myself again. My maid insisted that it would do me good to have my dinner in my study.

"Master too tired for big dining room," she said comfortingly. I nodded, completely loving the fact that someone was taking care of me once again. I had forgotten how comfortable my favorite chair could be.

I was still resting, when Kasi walked in with my dinner. Wisely, she had prepared a light meal, consisting of chicken soup, bread and some fruit. There was a fresh pot of strong black tea and I decided to drink it without any cream in it. The liquid revived me somewhat and I was able to take in couple of spoonfuls of soup. I waited to see if any nasty urges to throw up would manifest themselves. Since, that did not happen I nibbled on some bread and finished with eating an apple. I went to bed, very tired but not at all nauseated, for the first time in a whole week. I was too exhausted to inquire after Ciara's well being on that first evening back home. I was convinced that there would be plenty of opportunities to talk to her in the next day or two.

I woke up, feeling much better and almost myself again. I had Kasi's delicious ham and eggs for breakfast and topped it off with a cup of strong, sweet tea in my room. I worked for an hour in my study in the morning and afterwards took a short nap in the rocking chair, before going to lunch. It was then that it dawned on me that something was must be wrong. Ciara was not at her usual place at the table. Had things changed that much while I was away that she was not having meals at the dining room any longer? I realized how odd it had been that Kasi had not said a word about her last night or all morning. Maybe she was waiting for me to ask?

"Where is Ciara?" I said as calmly as possible. "She knows I like us to eat together."

"Oh," Kasi replied. "She's acting odd Master Richard and she no talk to me."

"Is she ill?" I asked wearily.

"No Sir!" She answered. "I no think so. Only for fortnight she eats in her room."

"She is spoiled, Kasi, that's all there is." I assured her, not quite certain that that was the case. I had just gotten back home and was already overloaded with troubles. I was getting tired of Ciara's changing moods. There was always something with her and I felt that I had enough other things to worry about. In just a couple of days I was due back at work and I needed to recover my health for that. I had no time, and no longer any desire, to indulge her childish behavior further. I had to find a caretaker to take her off my hands and do that as soon as possible.

The next few days did not ease the tension in my household. I realized that my housekeeper was right in her observations and precise in her descriptions. Ciara was indeed acting very strange and her wanting to eat alone was obviously just the tip of the iceberg. When I finally went to see her, in her room, she barely acknowledged my presence. I was so perturbed, that I decided to postpone the conversation about her future. I had enough time to let her know of my decision when everything was set. I had already begun the process of finding a suitable family for her, but that proved harder to accomplish than I had thought. To all potential caretakers I had described my "niece" as a nice girl with somewhat slow development. Truth be told, she was beginning to behave as a completely insane woman. She did not seem to want to spend any time with me and would not say one word whenever we were together. When Kasi and I would ask her something she would look at us as if all of a sudden she did not understand English. What I found even more disturbing was the fact that she had lost any desire to go out. It used to be impossible to keep her in the house for a stretch, longer than a few hours now she spent all of her time mostly in her bedroom. Sometimes, she would be lethargic and tired, at other times she would be restless, pacing about the room, and nothing could calm her down.

She began rearranging her bed every single night, but was still unable to find it comfortable enough to sleep in it. By the end of September she had decided to abandon her nice bedroom and moved into the cellar, choosing, for some reason, the darkest and dampest place in the house. I felt really compelled to lock her up in her bedroom, but she was acting so odd and our communication was so bad lately I did not dare. I could not possibly predict as to what she would do if I had. She seemed completely capable of breaking down the door or jumping out the window, if confined anywhere. I was worried she could seriously hurt herself, or others, if forced to do anything she did not want to do.

By mid October I have given up on trying to convince her to return to her bedroom. Instead I had ordered that her bed, and some of her furnishings, be moved into the cellar. Not that she was actually using her bed anymore. She preferred to spend the night on the rug on the floor, curled into a tiny ball. Most of her meals, she took in that misty place as well and she seemed more comfortable there, than in any of the clean, well-lit rooms of my house. She also seemed not to like visitors. That did not apply just to strangers; Kasi and I were obviously not desired companions either. On that point I remained firm and attempted to see her every single day. Nonetheless, Ciara would still not talk to me, or communicate in any other way what was actually wrong with her.

I was beginning to believe that she had lost her mind and my worry for her was vastly replacing my previous annoyance. I did not know if she felt I had abandoned her for three months and now was too angry to say anything. It was either that she had somehow forgotten all of the words I thought she knew or was simply refusing to use them. Both theories were worrisome and scary to me, yet there was little I could do to remedy the situation. My presence in particular seemed to make her feel edgy and I could clearly see that she had been behaving even more erratically when I was around.

Unfortunately, Kasi was no longer a desired visitor either. No matter how hard the poor woman tried to reclaim her old closeness with Ciara, it was all in vain. She was treated as an imposter, another female, whose presence was as threatening as it was unwanted. My maid was deeply hurt, yet still kept on caring for her charge with affection and without any sign of the frustration I was feeling.

The girl was spending her days mostly alone and seemed to have reverted to the unpleasant eating habits that she had in the early days of her arrival. If her meat was cooked at all, she wouldn't touch it. Her diet consisted now mostly of raw chicken and fish, hardly the satisfying, full nutrition for a young woman. She was drinking only water and only if it was room temperature.

The change in her once so active lifestyle was beginning to affect her physical appearance as well. Her swift movements were now a little slower and her figure a little rounder. Instead of running around like she used to, she would move very slowly. She was also taking naps quite frequently. Often, even when awake she would sit quiet and motionless as if she was listening to something that no one else but her could hear. It appeared to be something that was very important. Her other senses seemed extremely acute and alert as well. She seemed to posses an even increased ability to smell, or hear a sound that was many miles away. Many times she surprised me by leaving for the cellar, long before the mail man or other visitors had shown up at the front door.

The tremendous mental and physical change in her prevented me from pursuing my plan in talking to her. I did not want to send her away, at least not until I could understand what was going on. It was useless to talk to her in her present condition she would not understand a word I was saying. I could not send her away either, without having everything out in the open and her understanding that I had no other choice. I needed that clear closure of our affair and could not let her go until I had it.

By the end of October the only answer I so desperately needed was to the question of what was wrong with Ciara. I was slowly accepting that she had not gone mad nor had she began to suddenly hate everyone. As always before when it came to her, the answer was staring me in the face, only I was too much of a coward to see it. The thought had been keeping me awake at night. I was hoping and praying for it not to be the truth, but deep inside I knew it was There was no need of Kasi's already knowing glances or the passing of more time to be certain.

Ciara was with child. She was carrying our child and I was going to pay for my only indiscretion in the worst way imaginable. I would be condemned. This time there was no way out. It was just a question of time before her condition became apparent to everyone I knew. People would surely remember the infamous incident at the Colonel's villa, but I had convinced everyone, that he didn't touch her. I had done such good a job of it that people would easily realize that the only other man, having any contact with her was me. Welch himself confirmed my claims, that nothing indecent had transpired and people seemed to have accepted it. They would surely find out, that I was responsible. People always find out about such a thing and always assume the worst.

My entire world came crashing down on me and I was put there unable to pick up the pieces. The hardest yet to take, was Kasi's stringent disapproval of the situation. She seemed to have realized that I was responsible for Ciara's condition and she did not like it one bit. I had not fooled her for long and she wasn't willing to hide her disappointment in me. She expressed that with words stronger and harsher, than I heard her use speaking to anyone before. I felt too guilty to be willing to put her in her place and I could tell that my other servants had lost respect for me and suspected were already spreading the news. That aside, I was mostly hurt by losing Kasi's respect, perhaps irreversibly so.

Still, nothing she could say or do could make me feel worse, than I already had. I was crushed by the discovery of Ciara's condition and the only path left open to me was to wait. I was powerless to do anything else but wait for the complete and public disgrace to crush me and for Elisabeth to dissolve out engagement. I was to be surely banned from any respectable and decent home in Alexandria or London. I was most certainly to lose my job, my friends, and my entire world, as I knew it.

CHAPTER FIFTEEN

Ciara's condition was gradually becoming more obvious and seemed to be progressing in a normal way. Although I was not really prepared for such an eventuality I was expecting something out of the ordinary to happen. No one knew better than me that she was not like any other pregnant woman I knew. She was a daughter of Bastet, which was herself half cat, half woman. I had very good reasons to worry. Sometimes, when I would go to sleep I would have the dream of her giving birth to something unimaginably terrible, or even worse, a small black kitten. That nightmare was always the same and it never failed to scare me to death. The only thing that gave me some comfort was the thought that Ciara seemed to have the normal gestation period of human mothers to be. With Kasi's aid I have calculated that if she had conceived in May she should take to her childbed sometime around January. I could already envision the wonderful Christmas we were all going to have with the knowledge of the impending child birth, hanging over our heads. I could not even imagine what would be like if the fruit of her womb came into this world and it was some kind of a monster. As I had said before she was not like other women. I did not even know which and how big a part of her was even human.

Those thoughts and the intense discomfort I was feeling at Ciara's condition turned my affection for her into dislike, almost revulsion. Her odd behavior exasperated those feelings to the point I was avoiding visiting her every chance I got. The fear and superstition I had experienced at the first days of her arrival returned, and stronger than before. I was horrified of touching her or even seeing her, so I began keeping away from her altogether. The sight of her growing belly was a constant reminder of everything dark and base inside of me and the one crucial mistake I had made. That one came with consequences I couldn't possibly reverse or use in my favor.

I was beginning to really resent Ciara for what had happened between us. I was growing tired of having to always blame myself and felt she was just as responsible. It takes two for such encounters to develop in the way that it did. She was perhaps even more to blame since she was the aggressor. She knew exactly what she was doing! She had seduced me, I believed that and I had given in to her. She was the one who made our encounter possible and desirable with her act at the Colonel Welch's villa. Having to fight for her, did awake a certain possessive instinct in me, that I did not even know existed. I didn't force her into anything, which she did not want to do.

The enormous and silent patience with which she was dealing with her condition was annoying me. I was convinced that she wasn't capable of truly comprehending childbearing; she was too primitive for that. She was just accepting the position she was in, instinctively, and the same way animals adjust to changing circumstances in their lives. I was so determined to separate myself from her emotionally that some days I felt that there was nothing left of my previous affection for her. The hope of her dying and thus erasing the problem, sprawled like a nasty spider web in my mind. I was terrified, disgusted by this dark wish of mine, still never able to completely abandon it. Woman die, young, healthy women die from complications during childbed or just for no good reason at all. Then I could finally be free! I remembered hearing stories when a young child, whispered among the kitchen maids, and I wished I had listened more carefully. I remembered something about babies, that didn't want to come out and mothers fading away, because of a loss of precious blood. Some new mothers died because of ignorant and rough midwives.

Horrified at myself, yet strangely possessed, I could envision her death and was beginning to see it as my only salvation. If she died, I would grieve for her of course, but I could not help myself in realizing that such event would make everything a lot easier for me. There was still the matter with the baby though. I have not thought of that. What if it did not die with its mother during birth? One trouble would be replaced by another.

I had not fallen as low as to consider killing them both. I was not that evil. I was simply entertaining the idea of how their deaths would help me take my life back. I was trying to stop myself thinking and wishing those terrible thoughts. There ought to be another and better way out of my predicament.

Maybe, I could keep Ciara hidden in the house for the few months until the birth. She did not want to go out, at the moment anyhow. Only Elisabeth had inquired after her once or twice and she only did so out of courtesy and without any real desire to see her. Surely almost everyone else I knew would be more than happy to never see her again. She was too odd for them and had the tendency of making most people uncomfortable. The same way someone with a missing limb or a blind person does. Granted, a few young men were still interested in her, but I shall be able to keep them at bay. After the incident at Colonel Welch's villa, I had made it clear that any courting of Ciara was not to be tolerated. She was way too vulnerable for that.

It should be possible to keep Ciara out of the way after all. She had moved to the cellar of her own free will and I had nothing to do with it. I could once again, consider the option of sending her, this time with the baby, away. I can easily spare a small sum for her to live off of, faraway from everyone, and never see her again. It could work, but I had to tread very carefully. She must be confined to the house until giving birth. I shall refuse to accept any visitors for her sake. To any questions that were being asked, I was going to answer that she had fallen ill, with an unspecified ailment of course. I suspected that no one should care to investigate the matter any further, and I knew that in her condition

Ciara wouldn't rebel against her imprisonment. She had imposed it on herself by her own free will.

All of her old spirit and energy seemed to have disappeared, maybe forever. She seemed not to mind spending her days in the cellar, completely alone. Whenever Kasi and I visited she treated us with the indifference she had begun to display lately. It seemed forever, since she had step a foot upstairs or since we have had a meal together. She spent her hours, napping a lot or reading her favorite books, and seemed completely content with her own company alone.

With each passing day Ciara and I were growing further apart and neither of us was willing or knew how to change that. Although, she seemed inert and lazy to me now, I detected steely determination underneath her soft and rounded exterior. She did what she wanted, the way she wanted it, and not once did she ask for my opinion. An oddly independent creature had replaced the girl I once knew, and I was gradually beginning to realize that all the changes in her were not just skin deep, but a lot more fundamental, than that. The proof of that came one late afternoon when to my surprise she wandered into my study. Such occasions had become increasingly rare.

"Come in, sweetheart," I said gently.

She didn't reply faithful to her habits of late of not talking to me; but it was something else that captured my attention. Before, whenever she would pass by the oval mirror on the back wall, without viewing it different than any other flat surface in the room. Before, her reflection was to her nothing more than a strange woman that she needed to sniff to get acquainted to. This time it was different. She stopped suddenly, looking intensely and straight into the mirror. She didn't blink, but was just standing there, glaring into her reflection for a long time. Than she reluctantly lifted her trembling hand and pointed her delicate index finger towards the mirror.

"Ciara is there? Ciara is…I am…there?" She asked, slowly turning her eyes until they met mine.

"Yes! It is you." I said, unable to contain myself. "Sweet Jesus, it is marvelous, that you know that."

"Finally, you know!" I exclaimed very exited indeed, about the giant step forward she had taken. All the resentment I had felt for her lately, vanished in that one moment. I felt pride and satisfaction in her once again. Strangely, she didn't seem to share my excitement at all. She seemed busy observing herself, cautiously running her fingers over her face and clothes then touching the smooth, cool, glassy surface. She looked up to me a couple of times, a little confused, her smooth forehead now marked by thin, fine lines of confusion. I could see the intensity with which her mind was trying to grasp the unfamiliar, until just yesterday, notion of self. I wish I could say, that I knew how she felt, but I could not. It must have been something of a rebirth, the strange realization of that physical and spiritual unity. People usually accepted that togetherness when young children and that knowledge was a huge a stepping-stone in their development. They went over it at a reasonable pace. The shock must have been so much greater for Ciara, for she seemed to leap from the mind of a mentally disabled child to the complexity and depth of an adult consciousness. And somehow I knew that her condition had a lot to do with reaching that realization.

She ran away, slamming the heavy wooden door behind her, leaving me too startled to dare to follow her. I heard the squeaky sound of the cellar door closing, and I could assume that she had gone back to her lair. Did she really understand what just happened? I hoped she did, for what transpired had the power to turn her once and for all and entirely into a human being. My knees were shaking and I sat down on my chair, completely elated.

"I think, therefore I exist." were the words, echoing in my mind and I was repeating this famous axiom to myself, belittled by its ancient wisdom. For the first time in her existence Ciara had a realization of her own being, there was nothing more I wanted for her, nothing more I could give her. I wanted so bad to talk to her, to tell her that I understood the significance of what had happened. I wanted to tell her that I was there for her, yet how could I? It was too late. She no longer trusted me or needed me, and I was too busy, trying to get my life back. It was too late for us, but maybe not too late for her, for she was now complete, body and soul, and no one could take this away from her.

For the next few weeks I scarcely saw Ciara, for she never again visited me upstairs. On the rare days, that I forced myself to go into the cellar, her behavior was so calm and her eyes so full of understanding, that I could hardly stand it. I could wager that now she fully understood the actual and dual nature of our relationship and she hated me for it. Or was it just my guilty conscience that I could not make peace with? All I knew was that she knew that she was carrying my child, yet I wanted nothing to do with either of them. She also seemed to sense the love-hate mixture of emotions that I felt for her. She did not ask me for anything or threaten me with anything. As usual, she was dealing with the situation head on and by herself. Her courage made me feel even smaller than I already had.

Once again, I was too much of a coward to talk things over with her, to bring everything out in the open. All I did was to make sure that she was well taken care of. She had everything she wanted to eat and drink, the way she wanted it. If she chooses not to sleep in her bed, I did not flip out and force her. Seeing that my presence was disconcerting to her, I only visited when my need to see her became overwhelming.

Kasi was still tending to all of Ciara's needs and trying to spend part of each day with her. She remained steady, loyal, and affectionate as ever, like a mother, to my girl.

Pressed by the passage of time, I kept searching for an appropriate family to take her in, but was reluctant of approving anyone just yet. After all, nothing could be finalized until the child was born. That meant the family had to agree to take care of a mentally disabled girl and an infant as well.

I kept all information about my sensitive search very confidential, but had let my desire of finding someone be known among the locals. Finally my persistence paid off, when I found somewhat older Egyptian couple, willing to provide the needed care in exchange of a modest sum of money paid each month.

I met with them at their home and looking around at their spare rooms, I could not help but fear they were in it for the money. I guess that was to be expected. The man's name was Ahmed and the woman's Halide and they both looked prematurely aged from hard work. Their home was a poor farm in the country and they seemed to be ready to provide what was needed for an extra income. They didn't ask questions or show any change of mind, when I mentioned that the young woman was with child and there would be a baby, needing care as well. Ahmed and Halide expressed their willingness to take care of an ill mother and a child and mentioned they have always regretted not having children of their own. We bargained for some time over the money needed to be advanced, than settled on an amount agreeable enough to them and one I was able to supply without hurting financially.

At that point my personal impression was favorable enough and I decided to choose them as the foster family for Ciara and her baby. Anyone else I had seen seemed too shady to choose instead. I wanted to be rid of her, that is true, but I was still responsible of leaving her with a family that was decent. Ahmed and Halide seemed fine and even if there were in it for the money, they were country folks, ready to work hard for their bread and butter.

I could no longer wait to talk to Ciara about what awaited her, once the child was born. Mere weeks were left before that moment and I felt obligated to tell her of what was coming. Our conversation was way overdue. That Saturday morning after meeting with the Egyptian couple I took the steps to the cellar one by one.

"It must be done," I whispered opening the door, making sure that this time that I knocked first.

CHAPTER SIXTEEN

Ciara was taking a nap, cuddled with her feet underneath her inside of one of the big armchairs. Her left hand was resting on her belly; the right one was sweetly curled under her head. Her dark, rich mane of hair had fallen over the side and her peaceful face was exposed and for the first time in many months unguarded. Her mouth was parted and I could see the pink moisture on the skin on the inside of her lips. Narrow cracks remained between her dark eyelashes and her yellow irises were glowing true like tiny semaphores.

Unaware of my presence she looked happy; the expression of contentment on her face was so overwhelming that I remained completely still, frozen with the fear of disturbing harmonious rest. It has been such a long time, since I had seen her like this and, at that instant; I was struck with the abominable face of my betrayal. I was ready to abandon her and my child for nothing other than material gain. It did not matter how difficult my own life had been or how hard I had worked for achieving something in it, what I was planning to do with her was absolutely horrendous.

I kneeled quietly before her and put my left hand on the same place, she had kept hers, feeling the calm and steady pulsation of her blood in her belly. I could even feel the slight but persistent movements of our child inside of her. I was no longer disgusted or frightened. I did not want to take my hand away, feeling the baby move inside the womb was suddenly the most natural thing in the world. So I kept it there, astonished by the strength of that tiny life inside of her witch was decidedly declaring its rightful place under the sun.

She opened her startling yellow eyes, smiled and I didn't see in them any sign of bitterness, regret, or blame. I was holding back my tears and the hard lump in my throat was very slow to dissipate. I thought she hated me! I thought there was no bond between us anymore and I could let go of her as easy as I had of so many other things in my life. I could not have been more wrong.

I was mesmerized by the light as butterfly wings movements inside of her belly and kept my hand there for a time. I could not for anything send her or our child away, whatever the ramifications of my actions. We were bound by a bond so powerful that cannot be severed by nothing and no one.

I stood up slowly and softly kissed her on the forehead. I felt as if my soul was being separated from my body and it stayed in the room with the two of them. I was watching myself leave the room as if I was observing a stranger. Then, more than ever I needed time to think and decide on the course mi life was going to take. I was aware that there were not going to be second chances. I stepped out, blinded by the daylight, in so sharp a contrast with the murkiness of the cellar. It was a warm, glorious, sunny afternoon, as the autumn very often is in Egypt. The air was thick with the familiar aromas of various fried foods from the stands, present on almost every street in Alexandria. I could taste the salty, wet flavor of seawater, coming from the Mediterranean, lingering on my lips. I was walking, keeping a steady pace, observing the people move about their daily routines, as I was passing them by. As if for the first time since I had come to Egypt I saw her truly beautiful face. It was so colorful and happy and most of all full of life. Everyone around me looked busy and was moving about with seemingly a very clear purpose. I saw the happy face of a vegetable vendor that must have had a good turnaround that week. I noted the dark, rugged one of a field worker, on his way back home after a long and tiring day. I ignored his skin color and my imagination followed him to a small house where he would probably have warm dinner with his family. I visited several of little shops on my street, and with awaken acuteness, ruffled up all the fine garments on the stand. I enjoyed seeing the play of color against the light in silk so delicate, that if you rolled it up it could go through a ring. I admired the crispness of linen it kept one so cool in summer, it was no wonder it was one of the most favored fabrics among Egyptians. I was impressed by the elegant, smooth shape of a glass vase but equally savored the simple lines of the many ceramic bowls and cups. Suddenly, I was capable of seeing beauty even in hand weaved straw baskets or unevenly made lounge chairs. I was stunned by just how my five senses worked. As if I had been in a tomb or prison for many years and when out I was seeing the world anew and differently.

The sound of everything Egyptian was strangely comforting to my ears and the movement of the men, women, and things around me seemed very swift and harmonious. I could no longer envision only misfortune at the familiar sight of the blind flute player, but rather enjoy the joyful melody his instrument was producing. The sight of the beggar on the corner did not make me look away, for I could no longer see him only as desperate and disgusting. He seemed exotic and colorful to me and I surrendered in his cup all the change I had left in my pockets.

The fragrant twilight of the evening was already falling, as I settled in a small coffeehouse. I positioned myself just so I was still facing the dusty window. I could not look away from that New World that I had suddenly discovered. It was overflowing with wonderful smells and tastes. My coffee was served to me in a tiny porcelain cup, very strong and sweet, and I was sipping it slowly, allowing it to glide silkily down my throat. It was as if I had never tasted anything like it before and I was experiencing for the first time the velvety texture of the liquid and its intoxicating aroma.

I have lived in this country for a long time, but had somehow remained blind to its beauty and fascinating character and the friendly, wholesome nature of its people. It took a momentous moment in my life to understand, that Egypt was already under my skin with its message for a simpler life and unquestionable respect for old time values and feelings. It was quite an epiphany for an Englishman raised to believe in the superiority of his race, and the inferiority of all others. We were equal in everything that mattered after all, the people I saw today and I. We were fighting for happiness, fulfillment, for our place under the sun, only we chose different ways to go about it. Theirs was decidedly better. Many of the Egyptians I had once considered beneath me seemed happier to me than I was. Granted, their lives were often much plainer, yet they could see their goals clearer. They seemed more joyful to me when after a hard day's work went back to their modest homes then I was returning to my museum of a house. Granted, they were wealthy people among the locals too, but I was more impressed with the perseverance of the common folk. They needed so little to be happy, it was amazing to me. I did not know why I had been so unhappy for so long. Could it be, because I had often sacrificed my personal wishes for social advancement? Was it possible it was like that because I was alone? I used to think that I did not need anyone. Yet most of the people I saw on the streets had families and place they could call their own. It seemed to me that they had a purpose in life and clearly set rules, which to follow. They had probably never felt the fear of dying desperate and alone in their old age, for respecting and caring for one's parents was a crucial part of the Egyptian's mindset. Children were considered a blessing even in poorest of households. Death was not seen as an end, but rather as the beginning of a new and glorious life. Their time on Earth was spent the best way they could and death was a logical and not frightening conclusion to that. Many Egyptians still believed that doing good and living righteously would secure them a higher place in Heaven. As a result, they did not seek reaches the way people from other more 'civilized countries' did. A serene life, simple and free of excess was a goal achieved by many Muslims or Copts. I, on the other hand, could not think of any of my compatriots that I could actually describe as happy or even fulfilled. I was not that sure that the notorious cool English self control was to blame. We Englishmen were too concerned with conquering the world and one's social status to concentrate on what really mattered. We were ready to die for our country, and Her Majesty the Queen, and sometimes forgot that following one's duty was lonelier, than following one's heart.

I felt I had been lost in a labyrinth of doubt and selfish ambition for so long that I had utterly forgotten what was that mostly mattered in life. It was not all the material possessions, for you could not take them to the grave with you. Not your social status, for in the end you would be judged by how you lived your days, not what your title had been. In the end, what was important was being happy with the simplest, smallest things in life, ones that we so often take for granted.

I had been happier with Ciara than I have ever been in my life. If being with her required sacrifices I felt capable of making them. A part of me was growing inside of Ciara's belly and I no longer wanted to change that. I never knew that having a child could be so enormous of an event in one man's life. I wanted to do what felt right. I wanted to have a family and never be alone again. I wanted a real life and was finally ready to embrace it.

I would have been surprised by the sudden change of heart I have experienced that day, if I had not realized that it had taken control in me slowly and gradually. Ever since I had met Ciara we were meant to be together. And together we shall be. After all it was said and done that was what I really wanted. At that moment I avoided thinking about where we were going to live or for the potential scandal would most definitely deprive me of my livelihood. To everyone I knew, I had shamelessly impregnated my "niece" and this was not something to be easily forgiven or forgotten. Nor did I stop to think for the hurt my actions would probably cause Elisabeth. We did not love each other, so maybe she would not take it as bad as I thought she would. In any case I had no choice but to bring everything out in the open as soon as possible. I decided to make the situation public and stoically bear with the consequences. I felt strangely at peace; having made a decision I could live with and about which I did not feel torn.

The starry Alexandrian night had already fallen upon my return, yet I was walking home in leisure and calm I had not felt before after dark. I was invincible. There was no fear or doubt in my heart. Only love for Ciara and our child and ardent desire to do the right thing by both of them.

CHAPTER SEVENTEEN

My only remaining wish was of doing right by Ciara and our child. I had less then three months to prepare everything for his or her coming, and the first order of business was to find a doctor, a really good one. If I remembered correctly, Kasi had some prior experience in helping a midwife from her village and she would be allowed to help out. But for the delivery of my baby I wanted someone truly competent. The only question was whether to choose an Egyptian or British doctor. The former would probably have less of an education, the latter less of an understanding. I decided to write to a few people and see what name would come recommended. I had to do so fast, before the news of my indiscretion had spread. There was always Dr Makhi, of course, who as a family physician had delivered many Egyptian babies. Ciara might be comfortable with him, since he had treated her for minor ailments before. Suddenly choosing him seemed a given. I did not want to make my girl uncomfortable or hurting her anymore than I already had, by bringing a medic that was a complete stranger to her. I could only imagine how important it was for a new mother to be delivered by a doctor she felt at ease with. Besides, Makhi enjoyed a good reputation and seemed to have good expertise and was the right man to first be considered. I decided to send him a summons, as soon as I woke up in the morning.

From that day I had the epiphany to follow my heart, Ciara was free to go wherever her little heart desired. She chose to remain at home, yet as if sensing my change of heart began visiting me more frequently upstairs. She would still spend her nights in the cellar, but she was talking and spending more time with me. I did not expect miracles to happen I just hoped that we would be a real family soon. I had nothing to hide anymore. If anyone wanted to see my girl, heavy with child, they were welcome. I knew that my servants were already talking and soon there would be no need to declare anything. All I had to do was stay put and let things take their natural and inevitable course. I was sure the scandal would be enormous and was preparing for whatever was to come.

I was still obligated though to tell everything to Elisabeth. It wouldn't be right for her to hear about it from anyone else, but me. So, I invited her to a Sunday brunch at my house probably our last one together. In the note, I underlined the grave importance of the matter that I needed to discuss with her. She arrived on time as usual and in seemingly good spirits. The thin smile on her face vanished at the moment, she saw Ciara, over six months along, sitting on the couch next to me. She must have already heard something about it, but ignored it as malicious gossip. She kept turning her gaze back and forth between us incapable of asking the questions she must have had or voicing the terrible suspicions swirling through her mind.

"Please, sit down," I said trying to appear calm.

She shook her head in refusal without saying a word. She was just standing there, trying to compose herself, grasping and rubbing her hands so hard that I could see the pale blue marks on them.

"Elisabeth, there is something I need to tell you." I began, knowing that there was no good way to say, what I had to say and soften the blow. I stepped forward attempting to hold her hand, but she withdrew, shaking her head so hard that the plumes on her head were bouncing up and down.

"Ciara is with child and I am responsible for it." I said, without looking her in the eyes. "I deserve you despising me, but please, don't hate me. I can't bare it!"

She didn't answer motionless, stunned.

"Elisabeth, I beg of you…" She was silent and I saw a tiny crystal tear rolling down her left cheek. Than another one followed. Her chin began quivering while she sat; more like fell down, on the coach next to her rival. She was looking pale and disoriented. Desperate to do something, anything, to make things better, I rushed out of the room and returned with some water. She pushed the glass away, again without a word. She looked up, the moment when Ciara handed her a plain white handkerchief. Her facial expression changed and its angular lines became distorted, greatly altered by the powerful waves of rage and jealousy washing over it.

"You nasty, little whore!" She rasped. "You think that by stealing what's mine, you would become one of us?" Spittle was bubbling out of her mouth. I had never seen Elisabeth losing control like this. She always behaved as if she was born in control.

"Think again, little slut!" The veins on her neck turned purple and were bulging out.

"You are nothing! Do you hear?" She was screaming now.

I was shifting uncomfortably from one foot to the other.

"And you!" Elisabeth turned to me. I staggered back, suddenly terrified by the powerful rage of that tiny, skinny woman.

"Good for nothing, worthless man!" She spit the words out. "I hate you and I always will!"

She slapped me across the face with all her strength. I could feel her sharp fingernails, tearing through the delicate skin on my neck.

"The worse is yet to come, Richard." She said in a suddenly tired voice. "Do you hear?"

"It is nor over for the both of you." Elisabeth declared and waited as if she expected us to reply.

I nodded, unable to form any words or master any other movement at the moment. Elisabeth looked suddenly exhausted and very old. I had never seen the lines around her mouth before, nor did I notice that her neck resembled that of an underfed turkey.

"You will never recover from this." She said matter of fact, reaching for her gloves. She adjusted the hat on top of her coiffure with trembling fingers.

She was walking out and I wanted to stop her, I wanted so badly to make peace, only I could not make my body work. Her eyes, full of cold determination scared me more, then any of her angry words. She would never forgive me. Our engagement was over as well as any friendship we might've had.

I didn't know exactly what measures she would take for satisfying retribution. I only knew they would be severe. She would do whatever was in her power to have me excluded from any decent home in town. I wouldn't be able to show my face in any of the Gentlemen clubs or pubs around here. Not that I was going to attempt to go there after today. I didn't need the humiliation of being asked to leave. What was done could not be undone.

I turned to look at Ciara, expecting to see the joy of triumph over her rival on her face. Instead I saw compassion in her gaze, fixed at the door that had just closed behind my former fiancée. Then she looked at me and we saw in each others eyes the silent understanding of exactly what had passed. I saw her plain and simple acceptance of the situation just the way it was. I was already trying to do the same; there was so much I could learn from her. I resented the fact, that I had hurt Elisabeth, yet I knew I had not hurt her heart, but her pride. I was sure she would recover.

What was done could not be undone. I had the odd comfort of things being beyond my control and from that moment on taking an independent course of action. Realizing this made everything that I had to deal with, somehow easier. I no longer had to lie to my servants, my colleagues, or Elisabeth. What was even better, I no longer had to lie to myself. I had made my choice and weather it would be the right or wrong one in the long run was totally immaterial. My life was going to be completely different and I was ready to embrace whatever the future held.

The whole month of November I kept going to work, all the while feeling that those seemingly normal days were only the calm before the storm. The whole European quarter knew at that point of my complicated domestic situation. For weeks now, I was forced to bear nasty glances and excited whispers, whenever I happened to meet an acquaintance. People that I had considered almost friends, were not even talking to me now. Sometimes I would see people on the street or at work, which I had known for years that would respond to my greeting with the blank stares of strangers. I began spending all my evenings at home, my resolve a little shaky under the pressure of the unrelenting despise and scrutiny.

I decided to fire my gardener and my cook, for I felt they were nosing around too much. Besides, I did not know for how much longer I could afford to pay their salaries. I kept Kasi though. She remained as steady and reliable as always. I suspected her loyalty to be more for Ciara, than for me, but I was grateful for it all the same. According to my calculations, Ciara had conceived in May, therefore I shall expect her delivery of the child to be sometime at the end of January or the beginning of February. I was not sure about the exact due date, since my knowledge in such matters was pretty limited. I was too embarrassed of asking someone else's opinion on the subject. Besides, who could I ask, but a doctor and I have not found one yet. In any case I was sure the time was near and I was growing impatient for the arrival of my child. I was hoping it would be a son.

I did everything in my power to make Ciara comfortable. She visited me upstairs more often and we resumed having our meals together most days. Her diet was no longer disgusting to me; I knew that pregnant women often craved and ate the oddest things. Whenever she would take my hand and place it on her belly I was the happiest of men. I could often feel the movements of the child and they were so vigorous, that I knew it would be a boy. It would be splendid to have a son, one to carry my name. I shall name him Michael Adam Grant. It was thrilling to know that my blood would be flowing in my boy's veins and the Grant's name will carry on long after my body had turned into dust. I never again touched Ciara in the carnal way I had once before. I admit I still desired her. Some nights I could not sleep, I longed for her so much. Only this time I wanted more than her body. I wished for us to be together body and soul. I wanted us to be partners in our future life together. Unfortunately, the only way I knew how to be close was to go to bed with her. Yet, I had to bide my time. I was too scared of somehow hurting the baby. Besides, she seemed completely indifferent to the possibility of any physical closeness between us. With the passing of time, she began to act more affectionately towards me, but nothing compared to our old relationship. She seemed almost entirely enveloped in a world of her own and I did not wish to force her coming out. I was hoping that once our son was born she would once again have love and time for me. We would be truly together again. When that day comes, we would be unstoppable. I was ready to wait, understanding that our unborn child needed her complete attention. For my son, I felt ready to bide my time and wait.

On the 1st of December I arrived at work, only to find a written message that I was being called to my superior's office. The summons didn't come as a complete surprise to me. I knew I had reached a point in my life, where my personal choices would inevitably reflect on my professional ones. My career, the one I had worked so hard for seemed to be in real jeopardy. Why else would I be called to speak with the Britain's Counsel-General, which usually left his Cairo Headquarters, only to attend to very sensitive matters?

Lord Cromer had obviously found the scandal pertaining to me substantial enough, so he needed to attend to it personally. So, I was finally going to meet the gentleman I greatly admired but only so I can be reprimanded. I could wager he wanted to discuss my domestic situation and I knew there were going to be serious consequences for me after all was said and done. Because of my tremendous respect for his person it would be difficult to meet the Counsel-General face to face. I went over all the information I had on him in hopes to be somewhat prepared for that very important meeting.

Lord Cromer was a gentleman that had built a splendid carrier based only on skill and hard work. He had served Queen Victoria in India and his promotion in Egypt came as a just reward for the results he had delivered there. At first, his appointment was to be a temporary one but after the British presence in Egypt came to be of a longer duration he stayed on. Lord Cromer devoted so much time and skill to his position that he did the impossible. In just a few short years Egypt had a smoothly running administrative system and flourishing commerce. The Port of Alexandria was getting built and was already in use on several occasions. The country's almost non existing postal system had recovered and began functioning smoothly again after the years of Civil War. People began traveling again. Egypt was experiencing a rebirth and the Counsel-General was one of those responsible for it. Of course, he was not the only one whose hard work was so beneficial, but he was most certainly the driving force behind many of the developments here. His morals and integrity were impeccable and I knew that he wouldn't tolerate scandal in his administration, not even for a minute. During his occupation of the position as Counsel-General his people, including me, were subjected to firm, but fair treatment. There was no favoritism or ignorance, and to my knowledge no corruption, or system flaws that were present in several other administrations around the world. Englishmen were receiving better salaries and more privileges than any other Europeans, but they were also expected to set an example for honesty and gentlemanly conduct thereafter. I had never met Lord Cromer, but could claim to know plenty of him. Suddenly the prospect of his lashing despise, was unbearable to me. For a moment or two I considered going home, not at all that eager to face him. But I had run away from too many problems in my life. It was time to accept responsibility for my actions. This time, there was no one that could deal with it instead of me.

CHAPTER EIGHTEEN

I straightened my shirt collar and put on my dress jacket. My shaving mirror revealed a pale face and the frightened, watery eyes of a trapped animal. I crossed the long corridor and took the winding staircase leading to the Executive rooms. I knocked on the door of Lord Cromer temporary office.

"Enter!" He said in a steady voice. I walked in and to my surprise he rose to greet me. He did not shake my outstretched hand and I pretended to have raised it only to straighten my cravat once more. He gestured politely to the leather chair in front of his desk and proceeded to talking about the weather and the incoming wheat harvest, both common topics of conversation in Egypt. I wished he would get to the point, but had to endure the usual banalities, aware that he was not as eager as me to get everything out in the open. The matter was obviously way too sensitive to be discussed straight forward.

"I am going to be brutally blunt," Lord Cromer finally said. I feared he was not going to be, but nodded in agreement.

"Mr. Grant!" He said, avoiding looking at my face. "It has come to my attention that a certain young lady in your household is in the most unfortunate of conditions."

He waited for a reply, but I could not think of anything appropriate to say.

"I understand she is with child and that out of wedlock." He added impatiently. He was obviously trying to rouse some kind of reaction out of me.

"I also received a letter from Ms. Elisabeth Boyle," he continued, "with the shocking claim that you are the party, responsible in this matter?

"Yes! It is true," was all I could say, seeing the interest on his face being quickly replaced by revulsion. He moved his chair further away from the desk, as if in an attempt to put a bigger distance between himself and the pervert he saw me as.

"The lady is begging me to address the matter immediately and with the desirable firmness." He declared coldly.

"She is also referring to some old rumors that it is not clear where the girl, you insist to be your niece, actually came from?" He was regarding me now with obvious suspicion. He was maybe hoping that I had gotten the girl from some brothel and kept her in my house for my carnal pleasure. To him that was obviously more desirable, than her being a relation.

"She is not my niece," I finally said. The least I could do was clear myself of the suspicion of having a child on someone I was related to.

"I am the father of her unborn child," I added, "and she is innocent in that entire mess."

He did not seem to understand as to how Ciara could be innocent in matter such as this. He was not willing to listen to me anymore. Nor did he bother asking me why I had introduced her as my niece. What was the point? In his mind he had already convicted me as a terrible man, slave to his most basic urges and controlled by his lust.

"At least the girl in question is not a relation," he said after a short pause.

"Your conduct is despicable, all the same," He stated without addressing me by my name. He paused, drumming his fingers on the arm of his chair.

"The question is what to do about it?" He asked as if talking to himself.

I certainly had no say in it, I knew this much. My face was burning red of shame; I could feel the miniature drops of cold sweat forming on my forehead, and then falling down my temples. I was too upset to wipe them dry. I was not sure that I even had handkerchief in my pocket. I clenched my feasts, to prevent my hands from shaking. There was nowhere to run and there was no place to hide. I struggled to speak calmly and remain brief and to the point.

"Ms. Boyle has written you the truth." I said, hoping to end the interview.

"As I said, I am the one responsible for it and I am ready to face the consequences of my actions."

Lord Cromer was looking at me with a blank expression on his face, obviously still trying to determine the most appropriate course of action.

"Sir, there is nothing else I could or wish to say about the matter or the young lady involved in it." I said, now desperate to bring the meeting to its inevitable conclusion.

He was looking at me in complete disbelief and seemed miffed by my complete lack of remorse. I could very well understand his distress, yet there was nothing I could do about it. I stood up in the hope of ending this dreadful conversation. I might as well spare him the trouble of letting me go. That was all I could do to help him out.

"Lord Cromer, I presume, that in the light of this information you would request my resignation?" He nodded then said:

"We can't afford such an ugly stain on the reputation on one of our own. The administration is not strong enough to handle such a scandal," he said, unable to conceal anymore his feelings of anger and disappointment.

"I have worked too hard," he declared proudly, "to let a man such as you, to ruin all I have worked for."

He was growing angrier and seemed to be just getting started with a good verbal lashing. But I have had enough insults for one day.

"You will have my letter of resignation on your desk by the end of the day." I had been standing for the last minute and was now preparing to walk out.

Speechless for a moment, he waved his hand to point the way out. He did not stand up to see me off. The look of bitter disappointment on his face wasn't going to be the last one I would see in the time to come. How unfortunate that it was coming from one man I could truly admire. One of the few people whose friendship I wish I had and whose respect I wished I hadn't lost.

"I hope," he said quietly, as I had almost reached the door. "You are prepared young man, for the thorns, lying on the path you have taken.

I turned around suddenly scared, but also angry. I was tired of hearing this from everyone. I just wanted to be left alone.

"You will probably be banned from any decent social life and never work in your field again." He raised his voice, oblivious to my growing impatience with him and all the other terrible meddlers.

"Furthermore, I am afraid you will not be able to receive an appropriate engagement elsewhere in the country either, for word of bad reputation spreads quickly, regardless of my attempts to prevent it from happening."

"It is my affair," I screeched, unable to control my temper any longer.

"How dare you!" He said, standing up. "You betrayed your country and the institution you have once represented," he said haughtily. "You did not live up to your responsibilities as an Englishman."

"Stay out of it," I replied angrily, not addressing him by name either and reached for the doorknob.

I closed the door of the Executive office behind me, my anger subsiding and living in its wake tremendous relief. I remembered all the harsh words the Counsel-General had said to me, the bitter disappointment in his eyes. Lord Cromer did not need to warn me. I could well imagine the isolation, and humiliation, that awaited me in near future. I had already endured some of it and the worse was still to come. I was aware that it was going to be hard, perhaps even unbearable at times. Still, I could not detour from the path I had taken. So, his harsh words didn't truly achieve the effect he intended them to have. What happened was done, and could not be undone, that was becoming my favorite mantra. I was not sure that I would even miss the life I was about to give up, feeling as if I had never completely belonged to it. I was not happy before, maybe I could be happy from that moment on. I never felt fulfilled with all the material things I had possessed; perhaps I could be so if I had the perfect love and a good family. After all, a fresh start was just that, and whatever was to come to me, I was determined to accept with all the newfound strength of my just discovered philosophy on life.

Back in my office, I signed the brief notice of my resignation with big, bold letters. The pen tore through the paper, as I put the final point on my carrier. I had worked so hard for everything I had achieved, yet strangely I did not feel sorry to see it go. I was almost in a cheery mood as I walked out of the building, whose door I closed behind me and was probably never to open it again.

Walking home, I tried to evaluate my present predicament as rationally as possible. I was due to receive, as customary, six months of severance pay. I doubted that anyone would try to take that away from me, for they wished to see me gone and forgotten as soon as possible. If they fought me on this, the scandal would blow up even bigger, so I was pretty sure they would not.

For some time at least, I didn't have to worry about money. After that, I would have to find some other way to support the three of us. I still had my substantial art collection to turn to, if and when the day of real financial need arrives. Some of the artifacts were worth a pretty penny and I knew of plenty of people that would be more than happy to buy them from me, regardless of the state of my reputation. I was surprised to find myself willing and comfortable to part with items that used to be so precious to me. I was ready to make whatever sacrifices were needed to make sure that Ciara, and our son, would never want for anything. The uncertainty of the future didn't disturb me that much. For some time I had abandoned the idea of trying to control it or attempting to plan it further than just a couple of days ahead. I was ready and willing to live my life day by day. What was so good about knowing what would happen to you a year or two in the future. It only meant having the fragile illusion taking a hold of your life, something impossible for most people and most of all for me. All my life I've struggled to change my destiny, instead of accepting it the way it was meant to be probably at the very moment I was born. From that moment on, I was to lead a simple, modest life and to really believe that I would be provided for. I decided then, to never again set foot in any of the Gentleman's clubs or European hotels in town. I had to learn to ignore the annoying whisper and disapproving looks Ciara and I were most certainly going to be a subjected to. I didn't often before feel the need to be around my countrymen anyway. Many times I had to deal with their pride, unhealthy curiosity, and rudeness. I didn't expect their understanding and their resentment and chuckle did not hurt me anymore. Slowly, but surely, I have discovered a new kind of spiritual strength I didn't know I possessed, drawn from my honest conviction, that I was doing the right thing for everyone concerned.

My single thought, and only concern, was about Ciara and doing whatever was in my power to ensure a safe delivery of our child. Dr. Makhi had answered the little note I had sent him almost a week ago. He wrote that his schedule was extremely busy but he would try to stop for a house call as soon as possible. I hoped that as an Egyptian and a spiritual man he would pay no heed to all the scandalous talk around town. The latest rumor had been that I had picked up Ciara in the country and had paid fifty pounds to her father, so I cold take her with me. According that version I had soon after that made her my love slave. Someone, (I suspected Elisabeth) had already made the necessary research back home and it was quickly discovered with certainty that I had no living female relatives. Without knowing it, Ms. Boyle had helped me or I might have been in prison already. The laws were very strict when it came to punishing men and women caught performing adultery within the forbidden degrees of affinity. I guessed it was a little better for people to think that I had picked her off the fields, rather than I had taken advantage of my own niece. Still, the situation was dire enough and I hoped that news of my tainted reputation would not prevent the good doctor from treating Ciara. He was my only hope for my girl getting decent care when in childbed. I did not bother calling on any of the British doctors in town, for I was certain they would be only too happy to distance themselves from me and her. All I could do was wait and hope that Dr Makhi would finally come. I was determined be there for Ciara in any way I knew how.

CHAPTER NINETEEN

It looked to me as if Ciara was about to give birth to our son at any moment, but I knew that she still had almost two months to go until the delivery. It was already the middle of December and Dr Makhi still had not come to examine her as he had promised. I was very concerned about that. Granted, my girl looked the very picture of physical health and spiritual contentment, but I knew of plenty of women perishing while in childbed. Old people used to say, that women had one foot in the grave, when giving birth. I wrote to Dr Makhi again, but was beginning to worry that I had to find another solution for the situation we were in. Trouble was many of the Egyptian medics in the city of Alexandria did not even have a formal education. Of them, several had somewhat limited, only practical experience in childbearing. I did not trust their expertise and was forced once again to consider the unpleasant idea of summoning an English doctor. Perhaps one with a small practice would not be that concerned about delivering an innocent child born on the wrong side of the blanket.

For a few weeks now, I was looking for a way of making Ciara my wife. If we were to be married, maybe people would stop treating us as if we had leprosy. Granted, my carrier was over and we would not be able to live the high life. But maybe we could find our place and be accepted among plainer society. Yet even simpler families would be hesitant to socialize with Ciara and me if we were not legally wed. Other selfish considerations or social boundaries were no longer preventing this. The possibility of us entering in holy matrimony was exciting for me. I was anxious to marry her not only because it was the right thing to do, but also because this way I can ensure, that she can receive proper medical care.

The fact that she didn't exist on paper was the only serious obstacle in proceeding with this plan. She had no birth certificate or any other kind of document I could present to the proper authorities, so we could marry. I wasn't willing to take the chance nor did I have the knowledge for manufacturing false papers. If anyone was going to get caught doing something like that it would be me. I could just envision some overzealous administrator requesting an investigation and the possible consequences of that. A thorough inspection of such papers would prove them not genuine and with great ease. It was one thing, people talking, quite another having authorities getting involved in our lives. Too many things could go wrong in those circumstances. I had no probable explanation of where Ciara had come from, since it was already common knowledge, that she was not my niece. I would be declared insane, before I could even finish the story of her emerging from a broken bronze statuette. She would be taken away from me. The thought of loosing was more terrifying to me that any possible consequences coming from falsifying documents. Suddenly, I realized how easily all could fall into pieces. I could be her guardian before, because I was believed to be her uncle. Now that her actual status in my household was one of a questionable nature, I had to tread with extreme caution. It was better not to attract any more attention to her by marrying her for I was at risk of losing everything.

Mere weeks ago I was desperate to be rid of her at any cost. Now the idea of some autocrats getting their hands on her, made me sick to my stomach. I could not stand the thought of her being sent to one of those institutions, where mad or homeless human beings were housed in this day and age. I had once visited such a place when in London, and regretted it instantly. It was the most terrible, cruel, and barbaric place you can imagine, where people were treated worse than cattle. The vision of dirty, screaming creatures once called men and women still haunted me to this day. At night, they were shoved and roughly so in tiny, filthy rooms, sometimes eating and often sleeping in their own waste. The food was absolutely deplorable and there were rarely walks offered as well as any other form of exercise. My impression was that the basic needs of the mind and body were never really tended to. I also had the distinct suspicion that female patients were abused in other ways as well, judging by the bawdy jokes of the workers. I could never allow this to happen to my Ciara. Besides, I couldn't be of any help to her if convicted for falsifying papers and in a prison confinement.

Thus, I had to abandon the idea for the time being at least, of marrying her. I had the feeling that some day, and in some way, an opportunity would present itself and we could be husband and wife. Maybe that happy occurrence would somehow happen even before the birth of our child. There was little time left, but I was still hoping that something would bring this about. I did not want my son to be born out of wedlock. Only, I had no other way to deal with it, but to pray and hope. Fortunately, whether we were married or not, did not bother Ciara one bit. She took things as always in a stride while I was still often struggling to follow her example and accept life the way it was. It was hard, because I knew how cruel people can be, to children born out of wedlock. For the time being I decided not to worry and enjoyed the easy friendship we once again had. We had yet to resume our old closeness and affection, but she seemed more receptive and with ease with me every day.

I had reached a point, when I had begun to feel a tremendous respect for Ciara. I so admired the strength and calm she had displayed all throughout her present condition. Even as she was getting rounder and it was becoming obviously harder for her to move about, I never once heard her complain.

"How can you be so patient?" I asked one day as I was watching her trying to have a nap on a chair. She was no longer comfortable sleeping in bed or even curled up on the floor.

She looked at me as if she could not quite understand the question. Then said, "It is easy, Richard. I feel happy."

I knew that she was. And not because of me being there or even because she was with child, but because she was always happy with life, just as it was. Regardless of the physical discomfort her condition had placed upon her, she still was the perfect picture of health. She was simply glowing. When looking at her I could almost always forget the dreadful fear of something terrible happening to her. But I could never completely chase away the premonition of danger, lurking over Ciara. Ever since she came into my life I had the persistent notion, of her sudden and unexpected departure from it, one way or another. I was trying to convince myself that those fears were not justified; yet this didn't prevent them from always being present in the back of my mind.

And there was still the existing trouble of finding a suitable doctor for Ciara and the baby. The English medics I have written to already were perfectly clear in their refusal to help me or her.

Some used a very busy practice as an excuse, others straight forward informed me of their refusal to treat anyone in a household such as mine. That took care of that possibility. I then visited a few offices of local doctors, but saw nothing to make me less skeptical about their credentials. On the other hand, those medics seemed more than willing to treat Ciara and I was beginning to fear, that I had no other choice, but to select one of them. Dr. Hasid seemed cleaner and more organized that the others. His office had some resemblance of professional order and I saw several women in his waiting room. Some of them were definitely with child. He assured me that he had good experience in delivering babies and then requested to be paid his customary consultation fee of two piasters. I left his office weary and confused and decided to give some more thought, before hiring him as the man to deliver my child. Perhaps, I had no other choice, but hiring him. No one else was available.

Things came to a head the very next morning as Ciara and I were having early breakfast in the dining room. Kasi brought to me a tray with a note from Dr Makhi. It was written in the beautiful had writing I was already familiar with and he expressed his regret of not making the house call he had promised. He explained that he was taking care of a terminally ill patient that kept him very busy. Yet, all he could do was to make the man's last days more comfortable. He also said that he would stop by this afternoon for a complete examination of the young lady. I could not help but feel hopeful, that he had called her a lady. Granted, Egyptians always spoke with customary deference to any Europeans, but still it was a sign that the good doctor was not being perturbed by any silly rumors. Dr. Makhi was many levels above the so called doctors I had interviewed and visited. He had received a formal education in France and was from a rich, if not exactly noble family. I expected that the only reason not many Englishman were among his patients was because of their prejudice and snobbery. How could they possibly let a local man, put his dark hands on them? Nevertheless I liked him. He had treated me for some injuries before and had met and treated Ciara as well. He always behaved with the utmost professionalism and without asking any unneeded questions. According to Kasi, he possessed extensive expertise in his field and was pretty experienced in child delivery. To my horror, she insisted on telling me the rather long and complicated story of a young woman, which he had successfully delivered of twins easily and with no complications. Despite the fact I was not eager to hear that many gruesome details of the story, it made me feel hopeful that finally my girl would have a reliable medical care. I informed Ciara that Dr. Makhi was coming to see her this afternoon and she needed to prepare herself for the visit. I reminded her that if she had any troublesome symptoms in regards to her condition she needs to let him know promptly.

CHAPTER TWENTY

That afternoon I waited impatiently in my study for Dr Makhi to complete the so crucial examination of Ciara. It seemed to be taking a lot longer than I had anticipated. I knew how completely inappropriate it would be for me to be present for the exam, yet there was no place else that I wanted be more, at that moment. I was pacing from one room to the other, unable to relax and sit down, yet feeling not that much better from the exercise I was getting. The doctor had promised to inform me of his conclusions as soon as his visit was completed. Kasi stayed in Ciara's room and I was wondering whether to call her to me and inquire how things were going. It was definitely taking too long. He must have found something wrong with his patient's condition, why else would he need an hour and a half with her? When I looked at the antique clock on the wall I realized with a start that a mere thirty minutes had gone by since Dr. Makhi had gone downstairs. So he was not taking that long after all. I begun to worry then what the good doctor would make out of the fact that my young charge was residing in the cellar. Granted, I had made a decent bedroom out of the space, yet it was still a place where most people kept their wine and pickled herring at. No matter how I tried to better the space, it remained damp, dark, and misty.

After what it seemed a lifetime, there was a discreet knock on the door of my study.

"Enter!" I said, my voice trembling.

"Mister Grant," Dr Makhi said softly, coming in. "You have a very healthy young lady here."

He must have realized how worried I was and his professional demeanor and soothing voice were of instant comfort to me. The good doctor was of a small build with shiny black hair, smoothed neatly away from the face with some kind of hair oil. He did not wear a turban or the traditional long coat, so popular among the Muslim population in Egypt. His outfit was entirely European and was completed with a pair of eye glasses, perched high on the bridge of his long nose. When he felt he needed to make a point, he would take them off and hold them in his right hand while talking. His voice was as always quiet and confident. I noticed immediately that he did not call her my niece, nor did he refer to her status in my household in any other way. She was just a young lady and I was grateful for that discreet understanding of my sensitive situation.

"She is all right then?" I asked, feeling as if a huge weight had been lifted off my shoulders.

"Very much so," he replied his voice almost completely devoid of any accent.

"What of the baby?" I asked, my voice quivering.

"Baby is rather large and it is in the wrong position," Dr Makhi said cautiously. "Feet first, you know?"

"I cannot say that I do." I had no idea what he was talking about.

"The baby needs to be head down," he said, then seeing my obvious confusion added:

"We still have ways to go. Babies sometimes settle in the proper position in the last moment."

"What if he does not," I said, feeling frantic.

"Leave that to me," the doctor replied comfortingly. "Your duty now is to make the young lady as comfortable as possible."

"I will do so," I said walking him to the front door, after paying him for his consultation. His fees were by no means modest, but he seemed to know what he was doing.

"Do not worry," Dr Makhi said as if reading my mind. "She is one of the healthiest women I have ever cared for." He shook my hand and added, "I will be back again in one week. Do not worry," he repeated and closed the front door behind him.

I took the steps to the cellar one at the time. I was still not entirely convinced that everything with the future mother was as it should be. The doctor's remark of the child being in the wrong position had only confused me even more. I found Kasi and Ciara playing cards, comfortably seated around the small mahogany table and completely insensitive to my obvious distress.

"How are my two best girls," I asked playfully.

"We are fine," Ciara answered with a smile but did not even look up. I had the odd feeling that I was interrupting them.

"Can I join into the game?" I asked, hoping that if I spent at least a part of today with my girl I would feel better.

"Miss Ciara made up the rules," Kasi said hurriedly. "It is for only two people." She could not have said it anymore clearly.

The both of them certainly did not care if I was there or on the moon.

"Pleasant dreams, sweetheart," Ciara said with her usual underlining on the "r".

"Are you not coming to dinner," I said, realizing how pathetic it was for me to feel hurt for being left out.

"Miss Ciara wants dinner in her room," Kasi said defensively.

"I did not ask you," I replied angrily. They both looked at me as if I was being unreasonable. Was it too much to ask to spend some time with the mother of my child? I certainly did not think so. Ciara was about to give birth to my son, yet other than that we had little in common. And she obviously liked it that way. She was my wife in everything accept on paper, we had shared bed and board, yet I did not know her. We did not talk anymore; she was not asking me any questions, as if she knew the answer to everything. I could see that something was going on in that little head of hers, but what I had no idea. I knew that she had been continuously writing in that little diary of hers. I was never allowed to see any of its content. When I questioned Kasi about it, she assured me that all she knew was that Ciara was writing in it every day. Her life was monotonous, even boring. What in it was so interesting that she needed to put it on paper? The only possible explanation was that she was sharing with her diary her innermost thoughts and feelings. She used to share those with me. Granted I was amazed by the fact that she evolved thus far and was obviously having something of a spiritual life. Nearly a year ago she was like a simple animal, governed by all its basic instincts. Now, she was a thinking, and feeling, human being.

I would have been more proud of her progress, if I did not feel her remaining so far away from me. The ideal partnership, in body and soul that I had dreamed for with Ciara, was beginning to look to me to be only an illusion. I did not know anymore if things were going to change for the once our son was born. It was too often that I felt, as if nothing could bring back our old closeness and trust. I wished, I could find all the right words and ask for Ciara's love back and beg her forgiveness for all of my previous transgressions. I wished I could take back all the terrible things I had done. I was beginning to fear that I was, as usual, too late.

It was already early January and I was still hoping to find the right words to say to her. I was endlessly thinking of what to do to bring Ciara closer to me. Dr Makhi was visiting her now regularly and twice a week. On his last visit he did seem quite worried that the position of the baby had not changed as of yet. For the first time since he had started treating her he did not attempt to comfort me.

"The baby should have been in the proper position by now," he said, washing his hands. By the time January had rolled around I had earned the right to join the two women and the doctor downstairs in the cellar.

"What does that mean for her?" I asked quietly and smiled to Ciara, trying not to worry her. She did not seem to be in the least bothered by his words.

"It means the birth would be more prolonged, painful and dangerous," Dr. Makhi replied.

"We still have time," he then added, seeing the startled look on my face. "Do not worry." He whispered his usual mantra. But I was worried. I could not help it. The whole week I had a hazy, but persistent, premonition of danger. I also had the odd feeling that I was on the threshold of a major change in my life. At nights I could only get a few hours of sleep, constantly alert to the notion that something was about to happen, only I was not sure at that time whether it was going to be good or terrible.

I was not asleep on that cool Friday night either in the middle of the same month. I was just resting on my bed, when I heard the loud knock on the door. Somehow I was expecting it that momentous knock on my bedroom door. My heart rate quickened and I could almost feel the blood rushing true my veins.

"What is it?" I said, trying to control my voice.

"Baby is coming early," Kasi's voice was muffled by the thick wood.

"What?"

"Baby is coming," she yelled this time. "You must come!" She forgot in her distress to refer to me as her master or even call me by my name. I would have laughed about her lousy manners if I had not been so distracted. Kasi had never forgotten the customary subservience she owned to her employer before. I got dressed in a lightning speed and opened the door to the vestibule. Kasi was just standing there, all of her confidence and common sense, and had suddenly vanished. She was wringing her hands and seemed unable to do or say anything more.

"Go fetch Dr. Makhi!" I said, taking matters into my own hands.

She didn't move. Instead she put her hand on her throat as if to force some sound out of it. I felt she should be coping better. After all, what was happening was not some big surprise for any of us. Then it hit me. My son was coming, but he was more than a month too early.

"Hurry up!" I yelled. "Go!"

I was feeling very nauseous but exited too all at the same time. The moment I had waited so long for, had finally arrived. My son was coming into this world! In just a few hours I would get to meet him. He had changed my life, irrevocably, before he was even born. I was excited and very scared too. I was strangely scared that he might not like me. I could envision him pulling away from me in distrust and fear. Was it possible that a tiny infant could have likes and dislikes as soon as he was born? And the most important question of all was what if something goes wrong with the delivery? He was coming five weeks too early. I was too frightened to contemplate all the consequences that could come from that. I only knew that he was too early. Procreation was a risky enterprise for any woman in our day and age, and if she chose to undertake it, she had one foot in the grave already. And that was even when babies were positioned properly in the womb and did not arrive too early. The situation was a lot more complicated and potentially dangerous for Ciara.

CHAPTER TWENTY ONE

I hurried to the cellar, taking two, three, steps at the same time. I paused for a moment in front of the wooden door, trying to catch my breath, and struggling to calm down. I must not scare her; she had enough to deal with now, without me fussing over her, all worried and frightened. I carefully pressed my ear to the door. I did not hear a single sound in the spacious room. Kasi must have been wrong! It could not have started already. Ciara was probably just sleeping. I opened the door slowly and walked in, as quiet as a mouse. She was standing up and moving around and looked completely awake. There was something however, about her movement that made me stop and take notice. She was stepping with such a caution as if she was on a floor, inlaid with delicate eggshells. Her body was strangely stiff at times and her motions seemed difficult for her to make, yet she seemed unable to stay still or sit down. Her arms were tightly wrapped around her chest as if she was cold. But the room was warm, stuffy even. Her head was lowered, but I could still see her face. It looked calm and clear, its features enveloped by the concentration with which she was dealing with the ordeal she was experiencing. The soft glitter of perspiration on her forehead was the only sign of the enormous pain she was going through, for she remained silent. She kept on carefully walking from one end of the room to the other, pause for a moment or two, and then continue on her way. It seemed that every cell of her small frame would tense up by the sudden wave of every contraction enveloping her. In between them she would resume her instinctively measured movements, from corner to corner, until another painful spasm tore through her spare, little body. Her eyes were wide open and she looked at me, but I wasn't sure if she had actually seen me. Her breathing was irregular and seemed to almost stop during each contraction and turned into quiet panting in between. Her silent bravery in going through what seemed an enormous pain, made me burst into tears of confusion, love, and compassion.

"Please! Help her!" I murmured, not knowing who I was speaking to. I kept following her around the room, feeling utterly and completely helpless. I also felt very guilty for what she was going through. If I had left her alone that night, if I had just paused to consider the consequences of my actions, there would have never been a baby. She would have never had to go through this terrible ordeal. I needed so much to do something to help her I just did not know what. Maybe I can give her some wine or brandy, to ease the pain. She would never drink it though. Maybe some milk or water would do the trick. She is probably very thirsty. I ran upstairs and to the washroom. I filled quickly a glass with some water and spilled almost half of it on my way back down.

"Here, drink this," I said putting the glass near her lips. She turned her head away. I tried a few more times to coax her into drinking the water. I was sure it would make her feel better. Finally, she pushed the glass away with such a force, annoyed by me persistence, that I spilled its content. With trembling fingers I picked the glass of the floor and sat it next to the bed. Ciara had resumed her measured pacing, from one end of the room to the other.

"Sweetheart, come to bed," I tried to reason with her. "It can't be good for you or the baby to be hoping around like this!"

She stared back at me with such blank expression on her face that I could tell she did not understand a word I was saying. She kept on walking slowly and with clear purpose. I could see the muscles on her middle tensing up and releasing with each contraction and each time there was a shorter pause in between them. I must try again taking her to her bed. She needed to lie down, and then I can hold her hand and we can go through this ordeal together.

"Come to bed," I said convincingly. "You need to lie down."

Soft grunting was the only answer I received. She did not seem to hear me at all or comprehend what I was saying. I could somehow grasp that in the painful enormity of what was happening to her and there was no place left for anything else. I was not sure that she knew I was there or cared about it one way or another.

"Doctor, please help her! She is in so much pain!" I cried upon his bursting into the cellar. Dr. Makhi looked a little disheveled; his eyes were swollen with sleep. Nonetheless he was fully aware of the situation in just one glance. A trickle of clear, red blood found its way down Ciara's left thigh. I can clearly see it soaking trough the night shirt, creating the frightening shape of a little red rose. Then it formed a tiny dark puddle on the floor. At that moment she had stopped moving. Dr Makhi pushed me out of the way and with Kasi's help carried Ciara to her bed. She remained there, obedient and quiet.

"You need to go now," the doctor said, opening his bag. The look of his sharp, shiny instruments, whose dreadful function I did not even dare to suppose, made my stomach turn. I wanted to stay, I really did. His tools of the trade and the sight of the shiny puddle of blood still left on the floor were the two things that prevented me from staying. Kasi followed my gaze and hurried by me with a clean rag to wipe it off. But it was too late. I knew there was going to be a lot more of the terrifying red liquid, before it was over. I felt so queasy from only looking at the little bit Ciara had lost already. Staying for the birth was not only completely inappropriate I did not think I could be present without passing out. After some hasty words of comfort Dr Makhi requested my immediate departure.

"Have some brandy," he suggested as I was getting ready to go. "It should make you feel better. Please go and leave the rest to me."

Kasi stayed in the room and seemed to have collected herself enough in the face of the coming crisis. She was already warming up water and laying out some clean linen, obviously prepared ahead of time. I knew I could count on her. The good doctor and my maid looked busy, but knowledgeable and very confident. Ciara was lying on the bed, silent and motionless and so pale, that I concentrated on the movement of her chest to make sure she was still breathing. The painful, powerful spasms that were ravaging her body mere moments ago had stopped for the moment. I chose seeing her like this, not in pain as the comforting picture to keep in my mind, while I was waiting for the whole ordeal to be over.

I closed the heavy, wooden door behind me, but my legs were shaking so violently, that I barely able to stand, and did not attempt to go any further. I stayed at the bottom of the darkened stairway for a long time. The idea of a brandy was marvelous, if only I had the energy to go and fetch it. I did not. Instead, I positioned myself on a small wooden stool someone had left behind and stared at the door. Soon, I could count every crack in the wood, every shade of the paint, every facet of the polished doorknob. Once in a while I strained to hear the muffled voices of Kasi or Dr Makhi and guess as to what was going on. The waiting was almost unbearable, yet it was totally impossible to leave. I kept thinking of Ciara lying quietly in her bed, the sheet neatly tucked under her chin. She looked so small that it was impossible to trace the outlines of her body underneath. I felt so guilty for leaving the room and leaving her alone to go through the delivery of our child. Yet I was very aware how useless I was going to be had I stayed there. Instead of helping her I was only going to be on the way. Nevertheless I remained at her door. I could do nothing by standing there, but I decided I had to stay. The least I could do was to be near if the patient or if the doctor needed something. Such a need might very well arise and my other servants were gone for good. I kept telling myself that everything would turn out well. It was bound to. Ciara was very possibly the strongest, healthiest woman I've ever known. There was certainly no valid reason to worry about the outcome. Dr. Makhi had told me so many times and I struggled to believe him.

It was too dark and I was unable to follow the time on my pocket watch, but assumed that it must be four or five o'clock in the morning already. The hallway was saturated in almost complete darkness with the exception of a distant candle light coming from upstairs in the kitchen. I had thought about going and fetching a candlestick for me, but the idea of illuminating the place of such a spiritual torture for me was rather deplorable. Besides, I could not bear abandoning Ciara's door for even a moment. I had pressed my ear to the door a number of times, but all I could hear was muffled voices and clinking of what I assumed were medical instruments. Not once did I dare to look in. I knew too well that the place of the future father was certainly not in the birthing chamber. Only doctors and midwifes belonged there. But it was not that which prevented me from cracking the door. I was completely terrified of what I might find if I did. For the moment I could convince myself that if I did not see or hear trouble, then there was none to be found. I could almost believe that it was normal for the whole lengthy affair to be of natural duration. I almost believed that the doctor was simply too busy to peek out and let me know how was everything going and that Ciara and the baby were fairing just fine.

In short, I could almost convince myself that everything was going exactly as planned. I was straining to hear the baby crying, thinking that this could be my clue that everything was over and done with. Then I could go in and kiss my exhausted girl and finally meet my son. But I had not heard a baby crying yet. So all I could do was keep on walking, exactly three steps to the right wall and exactly three to the left. Henceforward I had begun ignoring the stool, feeling too anxious to sit down. On the other hand, I was growing so tired from the pathetic and repetitive form of exercise I was involved in, I was ready to collapse. It was still better to be doing something and walking was the only thing to do in the tiny hallway.

It was probably for the best that I could not see the time on my pocket watch. I was growing more frantic with each and every passing hour. Dr Makhi had arrived sometime around ten o'clock last night. It must have been at least five in the morning by then and still no news of any kind. I could tell it was getting closer to morning, because a narrow strip of the midnight sky I could still sees through the tiny window was becoming lighter blue. There was still a little time left to sunrise yet and every passing minute was becoming more frightening than the last one. I could not shake off anymore the dreadful feeling that something had gone terribly wrong. It was eating me up and becoming stronger all the time. Seemed to me that I have spent an eternity in this place, in the darkness, and alone. From what I thought I knew of birth and delivery, the whole ordeal should have been long over. Even thought I knew it might take longer for a new mother to deliver her first child, it should have been done with. Ciara was too healthy to have any difficulty and no one knew, better than me, how strong she was. She was not like all the other women, members of the weaker sex. She was a fighter and she had proven it many times by always landing on her feet. She was the Daughter of Basted, and as such, nothing bad could happen to her. Ciara was half cat, half woman and must have a few lives left in her yet.

I kept on walking about, for the movement it seemed the only thing able to offer at least some relief to my troubled mind. One moment I was scared of losing her, in another, I kept thinking how strong she was and felt she could survive anything. The worst still was the complete helplessness I felt in the present situation. I had no way of doing anything and making it better.

The gentle twilight of the cool January morning soon colored the glass of the tiny window in a very light blue. I was still where I had been for the whole of that long and dreadful night. I was pacing at the foot of the stairs, desperate for some news, but too scared to find out for myself if there was any. By that time, I had realized with a terrifying and unshakable certainty that something truly bad had happened. The only thing I did not know was whether it was with Ciara or the baby. Shaken up, I suddenly remembered some the evil thoughts I had gone through at the beginning of her pregnancy. Maybe, I have not heard the cry of a baby, because she had not given birth to a human child. The doctor and Kasi would still be in shock from witnessing the birth of a monster. After all I was the only one who knew of Ciara's true origins. Maybe it was a human child, but it was stillborn. Or maybe they had both died and the witnesses to the death were too weary to notify me of it. I kept staring at the closed door. I felt completely capable of burning holes in the wood with just my eyes. Yet, I was still lacking the necessary strength to take the needed few steps and go in. I truly didn't want to know what had happened; that way there was still some hope left in my heart.

CHAPTER TWENTY TWO

The door opened with a loud crackle and Kasi peeked out. I did not need to see her tear streaked face to know she was bringing with her very bad news.

"Master Richard, she is not well". She cried.

I paused trying to take in the full meaning of her words. She was obviously waiting for me to say something. I cleared my throat, for a moment, unable to force any sound out of it.

"What happened," I said weakly. I felt that I was stranded in a terrible nightmare and wanted desperately to wake up.

"Doctor says she is bleeding inside!" Kasi was explaining between sobs. "He says she going to die!"

"Going to die, die!" She screamed the last word over and over again until I felt ringing in my ears, than stopped suddenly and heavy leaned against the wall. She stood there for a moment, reminding me of one of those flies stuck in a herbarium in entomology class. Then she started falling down, her hair and clothes, making the oddest sound scraping at the wall. I was too much in shock myself to catch her on time and she ended up on the floor; a heap of flesh silent and motionless. I somehow managed to pick her up and put her on the stool, and she remained there, rocking back and forth deep inside of her sorrow. Suddenly, she took her hands off her face and revealed it all red and puffy. It was so sad and distorted that I realized that she must have known for a while now, that Ciara was dying. She stood up slowly and softly gestured to me to step into the room. For a moment I could not move. I kept thinking, hoping that I was just dreaming a terrible dream and all I had to do was wake up and I would be safe in my own bed. Dr. Makhi rushed out, mumbling, explaining to me that he had tried to maneuver the baby manually, but was unable to do so.

"She is losing too much blood and the baby is probably dead already." He said all that with a voice no longer calm and professional. It was quivering and full of desperation and guilt. I pushed him aside and walked into the cellar. I did not need his explanation any more. I already knew exactly what had happened. I had wished for Ciara's death once long ago and now the vengeful gods were granting my wish. She was to disappear from my life as suddenly, and as dramatically, as she had entered it.

"Leave the room!" I said softly. They had followed me into the room and I found their presence useless and annoying.

"Please!" I insisted at Kasi's attempt to plead for her staying inside with me.

"I must be alone with her," I said dreamily. "She cannot go without me saying…There is so much I need to tell her." She nodded, covering her eyes, but I could not allow myself to be disturbed by her grief. There was space in my heart for only my pain and no one else's, and it felt so heavy from its weight. My only desire was to stay with Ciara as she was slipping away. I could not let her die alone as I had left her so many other times. I did not have a life without her; this much I knew as I knelt next to the bed, holding her cold hand in my palms. I would never again be able to warm it up. She was as pale as if there was not a single drop of blood left in her spare body. Her eyes were closed and the lids looked purple and almost transparent, but she was still breathing all though interrupted and shallow. The horrific contractions tearing her up had finally stopped. I was thankful for that.

"Ciara, my darling," I called out her name softly, trying to ignore the loud cries of my maid behind the door, or the noise made by Dr Makhi while he was putting away his instruments back in his bag in the hallway. I registered with indifference that he had left without even saying goodbye. I did not care. My girl was dying and there was nothing I or anyone else could do about it anymore. All the love, struggle, and pain we had gone through since she had come to me was all for nothing. Once again, I had been too much of a coward and my participation in that dreadful night was just as insignificant as it had been always been. My role was secondary and my coming to the stage late as usual – the story of my life. I could not possibly describe the nature of the power my girl had over me, I only knew that I loved her and my heart was breaking. I knew I could never put it together again.

Suddenly Ciara's entire body began trembling! She somehow lifted her head and shoulders off the pillow and let out a horrific scream! It was the only one that I have heard her make that whole, dark night. It was immediately followed by unexpected and very frequent, violent contractions. She could not even take a breath between the waves of excruciating pain that had once again reclaimed her body. I wanted to shout words of encouragement and love to her, to tell her what she meant to me, but there was no time. Everything was happening too fast. My throat was painfully raw, my jaws clinched so tight, that all I could manage were indescribable sounds, not resembling any words I had ever heard. In the next few short seconds, Ciara was shaking, but she didn't appear to be suffering. Through all of my horror and confusion, I grasped at the absurd thought that maybe not everything was yet lost. It looked that my son would still be born after all. The doctor must have been wrong! Kasi had been wrong for listening to him as well. It simply took a bit longer, that is all! The baby must have turned into the right position in the end and it was now coming for certain.

I made myself stand at the foot of the bed. This time I was going to be there for her, no matter what. A tiny, elongated head, covered with blood and slime, the hair matted on the skull was slipping out of her. It was followed by two tiny shoulders and arms folded tightly around the chest. The rest of the body began slowly squeezing out inch by inch, like a serpent changing its skin, than it suddenly stopped. For a moment it seemed that the little creature had changed its mind and decided not to abandon its mother's womb. Or my girl was so deadly tired, that she was unable to bear down and push him out. I struggled to compose myself and use my very limited knowledge in matters such of babies and deliveries. The doctor had been useless in the matter and besides he had already left. Kasi was just outside the door, yet suddenly I had the overwhelming urge to do everything alone. I had no one else, but myself to count on. I reached down and began to gently pull the slippery, frail body towards me and out. My hands were trembling, so it took several attempts for the little creature to come into this world. I wasted many precious minutes in attempts to cut the umbilical cord. It was amazingly durable piece of flesh; luckily I found a pair of surgical scissors that Dr. Makhi must have forgotten. Finally I was able the separate the newborn from its mother, but worried for the blood, oozing from the navel. I looked franticly around for something to tie the navel up with and all I could find was a narrow silk ribbon wrapped around small red book, left on the night stand. The newborn was covered in so much blood and slime, that I was unable to determine for certain its sex. All I could tell was that it had two arms and two legs. I was grateful for that. There was no time to wash it out or count its toes and fingers. I wrapped the baby, as it was, in a clean, soft blanket that I had found next to the bed. Some unexplainable instinct made me place on the breast of the new mother. She must have felt its sweet weight, yet to my surprise did not reach to touch the child she had waited so long for and suffered so much give birth to.

It was then that I noticed for the first time since I had walked it that the room was in complete disarray. Dirty linen and spilled water covered the floor. I saw pots and bowls in an untidy heap in the far corner. The sheets were soaked in blood through the mattress. Even the pillow case was now colored in bright red, instead of white. I had never realized there was so much blood in the human body. The enormous bed was covered in it. I stood up just in time to vomit on the side of the bed. I tried not to make too much noise doing this; I did not want to disturb her.

When I next looked at Ciara she was lying completely motionless and silent. God help me, she already looked dead and gone. I shook her by the shoulders unable to accept this, wanting to wake her up, to revive her somehow. She was like ragged doll in my hands. I laid her carefully back down again and laid my head on the bed. I could feel the wetness of her blood under my cheek but did not move. I grabbed a hold of her lifeless hand with such a force, that I left blue marks on the pale flesh. I know I must have fallen on the side of her bed a second later, only I did not feel my head hitting the stone floor. Somehow, I was still holding her hand when I came back to my senses. I wished I could not cry. The terrible tightness in my chest might dissipate, melt from the moisture. Still there were no tears, only dry heaving sobbing coming out of my mouth until even they finally ceased as well.

Suddenly I heard a weak, distant wail but I could not register where it was coming from. Then I realized it was coming from the tiny, disheveled bundle lying next to the body of my Ciara. I stared at it for a moment or two, annoyed by the lonely sound in the otherwise quiet room. I felt spent and numb. Then a movement so light that I thought I had imagined it, burned through my fingers, reached my heart, and I cried out in disbelief. Ciara opened her eyes just a crack, the mere motion of it seemed to extinguish the last spark of life in her body. She looked at the baby for a long minute, and then moved her eyes on me. Her hand moved aside, she drew it up shakily pointing to the simple jewelry box I have given her long ago. I had not given her any jewelry ever and I suppose she was keeping some trinkets in there that were special to her. The little red book, whose ribbon I had taken was standing right next to it. Both items were carefully positioned on the night stand as if they were about to serve a clear purpose.

"This is for her!" She said. "It is for my daughter." Her eyes were still fixed on mine. In that instant she seemed to know, to understand everything that had happened and was going to happen henceforward. Perhaps she always had known. Then ever so gently she enfolded my hand with hers. I felt her fingers lightly squeezing mine. I could tell that there was more she wanted, and more that she needed to tell me, but could not. Her time was running out. Then just like that she was gone and I knew beyond a shadow of a doubt, that this time she was not coming back.

I closed Ciara's eyes and gently positioned her limbs, so she looked as if she was only sleeping. I remembered the old superstition of putting coins on the eyelids of the deceased so they can pay the person guarding the gate to heaven to let them through.

It was a pagan belief to be sure, nonetheless I dug out couple of silver coins I still had in my pockets and laid them on her closed orbs with trembling fingers. I was strangely mesmerized by the steeliness, which death has given to her body and everything around it. It seemed as though time had completely stopped, and I liked it like that. As if, sleepwalking I went to the nightstand and picked up the jewelry box she was so adamant to show to me. I lifted the delicate hatch and opened it carefully. It was almost completely empty. There was only a pair of simple gold earrings neatly place on the bottom. I recognized them right the way as the ones she had on in that unforgettable night, she had come to me. I could cry now, for everything that was and could have been between us, but the tears didn't bring me relief, only enormous void in my chest. I lifted my head, disturbed by the annoying sound interrupting my grief.

"What the bloody hell is this?" I asked out loud. I heard the distant cry again, growing more persistent and ear piercing with each passing minute. I instinctively walked toward the sound; thinking that I only wanted to silence it, stop it somehow. I reached slowly for the loud bundle lying next to the body that had given her life, so the child could live. I unfolded the blanket and began sponging off the blood and slime away, mechanically and with the water that was already in the room. The water was cold and the newborn shivered and cried even louder from the chilling exposure to the outside air. I could recognize now with certainty that it was a little girl. Her dark hair was long, curling at the ends and although her eyes were closed I could wager that they had the striking color of yellow sapphire. I wrapped my daughter in clean linen sheet and laid her once more next to her mother. She was not crying any longer and seemed warm and content from my touch.

Ciara's diary, the little red book was still on her nightstand. I supposed I can read it now; she would no longer mind me knowing her innermost thoughts and feelings. Then, I remembered that the diary was one of the items she had pointed to as well, just before her death. She had clearly indicated that both items were intended for our little daughter. I opened the book carefully. It was filled out with the young woman's handwriting. The letters were large and clumsy as if a child had written them. The last entry was from yesterday the seventh of January. It was scrawled with a shaky and uncertain hand, yet it was easy to read.

"My daughter," It began.

"I leave a rich inheritance to you, one that comes with much power but also with big responsibility. You are a child of Bastet, but most of all you are my daughter and because of that your life will be easier, than mine had been.

I do not know where or when or how I was born. I do not know what my name truly is, but the one given to me in this world is Ciara. I am a Daughter of Bastet, but I abandoned my mother, the moment I wished to become a human being. I wanted it mostly for the love I felt for your father, but for myself too. I wanted it more than I ever wanted anything. And now I am truly a woman inside and out. The powers The Goddess had given me, I never used. Use yours and never fear them.

Love your father. Love is everything he needs, whether he knows that or not. Now, that that my time has come I can not only love him, but I have forgiven him.

8Th of January 1889.